SPIRIT WORLD

RESTLESS SPIRITS

SPIRIT WORLD

RESTLESS SPIRITS

BRUCE COVILLE

Hodder
Children's
Books

a division of Hodder Headline plc

To my sister, Patti

First published in the USA in 1996 as an Archway Paperback
entitled *Chamber of Horrors: Waiting Spirits*,
published by Pocket Books, a division of Simon & Schuster Inc.

First published in Great Britain in 1998
by Hodder Children's Books

A Catalogue record for this book is
available from the British Library

ISBN 0 340 71458 1

Typeset by Hewer Text Ltd, Edinburgh
Printed and bound in Great Britain by
Mackays of Chatham, Kent

Hodder Children's Books
a division of Hodder Headline plc
338 Euston Road
London NW1 3BH

Introduction:
STEP INTO MY
CHAMBER

At the end of the street stands a strange old house. You check the address on the piece of yellowed paper you hold in your trembling hand. Yes, this is it. You've come to the right place. The chamber of horrors is straight ahead, waiting for you, waiting for you to enter.

You climb the rickety steps. The door creaks as you open it. A cobweb brushes your forehead, and from the corner of your eye you notice something with more legs than seems natural scuttle into the darkness.

In the shadows ahead lurks your host. He utters a low, mysterious, bone-chilling laugh.

And suddenly you wonder if this is really where you want to be.

You'd better turn back now, while you still can,

because your journey into the heart of fear is about to begin.

What's this? You're going to stay?

Well, then—welcome to my nightmares. I've been studying fear all my life. First my own fears, the creeping terrors that came at night and left me staring into the dark, wondering what lurked in the closet, under the bed, waiting to grab me, take me, carry me away. Then the fear I found in movies, and books, and (sometimes most delicious of all) around campfires. I experienced the thrill of the chill, and at the same time yearned to learn to do the same thing to others— to you, dear reader: to make your blood run cold with fear.

Let me explain my theory of fear, my preferences when it comes to terror.

First, I think you need a good laugh once in a while. It makes the terror that much worse.

Second, I think horror and adventure are a perfect mix.

Third, I'm not crazy about buckets of blood. It's easy to fling them around, but it doesn't take much skill, and what you get is as much disgust as true fear. If you're looking for loads of gore, you've come to the wrong place.

I'd rather take you into a long dark hall where you know something horrible is waiting; lead you down that hall, lure you along, so that with every step you want to turn and run, yet find that you can't because you have to go on, to see what happens.

At the end of the hall is a door. And behind that door is a mystery that fills you with dread; something you long for, but fear.

You want to turn. You want to run.

But your hand, almost of its own will, reaches out to open the door. . . .

The lights go out. The door swings open.

And now it's too late to leave. You've entered the first room of the Chamber of Horrors.

The door slams shut.

Welcome to my nightmare.

Bruce Coville

PROLOGUE

Carrie Halston was playing in the garden when she saw something she shouldn't have, and that was what cost her her life.

It was a beautiful day in August. The sun was high and hot—too hot for the frilly dress Carrie's mother had insisted she wear. Through the windows of the house she could hear the strains of "Beautiful Dreamer" drifting from the gramophone her father had brought home the week before.

She liked the song. It was sad, it seemed to her, but very pretty.

She picked a handful of daisies from the formal planting and went to look for her mother, wondering when her big sister would be finished making the lemonade.

The fish pond attracted her attention, and she

stopped to stare into its murky waters. She loved the great shimmering fantail goldfish, their bodies as large as her hand, their tails like bridal veils trailing out behind them. After laying the daisies on the bench, she went to get the little jar she had hidden out here the week before.

It was so much fun to watch the fish eat.

She sprinkled some food on the water and pursed her lips with delight as the golden figures floated to the surface, graceful and ghostlike. Kneeling at the edge of the pond, Carrie reached for one, knowing she could never catch it, but unable to resist trying anyway.

Suddenly she slipped, and her whole arm plunged into the pond. She pulled it back as if she had been burned. Now she had done it. Her mother would be furious because she had spoiled her pretty dress.

A lump of panic forming in her throat, she replaced the cover on the jar and returned it to its hiding place.

What should she do?

She gathered her daisies and looked around frantically.

Near the summerhouse was a hiding place, a clump of bushes where she would be safely out of sight until her sleeve had dried. Then maybe she could brush away the incriminating green.

Carrie hated it when her mother was angry with her. Mommy was so lovely, so pale and pretty. But when she was angry her eyes grew wide and frightening, and her breath began to come fast. Sometimes she would even faint. That was what Carrie hated most of all; she felt guilty whenever it happened.

Parting the branches of her secret place, Carrie stepped into the cool shade. She had sneaked an old pillowcase out here early that summer; now she spread it on the ground so she could sit without getting her dress any dirtier than it already was.

She laid the daisies on her lap and began to wait.

A ripple of laughter from the summerhouse made her look up. It was her mother's voice. She sounded happy. Maybe she was in a good mood!

Carrie looked at the daisies. They were starting to wilt. What if they were ruined before she could give them to her mother?

She listened carefully. She heard a man's voice, low and soft. Then her mother's sweet laugh again.

Maybe Mommy wouldn't be angry after all. Maybe she would like the daisies so much she wouldn't say anything at all about the dirty sleeve.

Hope rising in her heart, Carrie Halston parted the bushes and stepped into the sunlight. She let out a little gasp.

"Carrie!" cried her mother, her voice filled with dismay.

Then the other one began to chase her.

Still clutching the daisies, the little girl ran back along the path to the fish pond.

"Mommy!" she cried. "Mommy, help me!"

But there was no answer.

It would be more than fifty years before Carrie Halston's mother answered her.

1

Lisa Burton tiptoed down the hallway of the old house, carrying a bag of potato chips, a two-liter bottle of orange soda, and a pair of plastic cups. Her cat, Smokey, wove between her feet as she walked, barely missing being stepped on.

"This is the dumbest vacation in the history of the world," Lisa muttered as she entered the bedroom she shared with her little sister.

Carrie, seated at the card table in front of the Monopoly game, rolled her eyes in agreement.

The radio on the nightstand was playing the summer's big hit song, "The Corridors of My Mind." Only the sound was set so low—in order not to disturb their father—that Lisa could barely make out the words, which was driving her crazy. She wanted to crank the volume and cut loose.

5

Outside the rain continued to fall in a slow drizzle.

Lisa sighed as she sat down to the game—their eighth in five days. Five days of rain. Five days of being trapped in a house she had never wanted to come to, with a kid sister who was okay but, after all, only a kid, and with a father who was acting more like a caged bear by the hour.

What a way to spend her sixteenth summer!

It wouldn't be so bad if her father was actually enjoying himself. After all, they were supposedly doing this for him. But he was as cranky as she had ever seen him.

Maybe this book of his wasn't such a good idea in the first place, Lisa thought—not for the first time. Nor the last. After all, Martin Burton was a professor of physics, not a science fiction writer. But for years he had had an idea for a novel he wanted to write. Alas for him, as a family man he always spent his summers teaching extra classes to earn additional money—leaving him little time for any writing other than the academic papers he had to produce to fulfill his requirements at the university. So he had been delighted when he had finally gotten a raise that would free him to spend the summer working on his pet project rather than teaching.

Then Mrs. Burton's mother, Dr. Alice Miles, had called with the news that she had rented the house she used to summer in as a girl, and wouldn't it be wonderful if they could all spend some time together on Sayers Island where Martin could work in peace and quiet, away from the distractions of home?

Without consulting their daughters, Mr. and Mrs. Burton had decided it was a great idea. Before Lisa

6

knew it, she had been yanked away from her friends for the entire summer.

Actually, it was one particular friend she would really miss. Things had just been starting to click with Dennis Rodriguez when she had had to leave. Lisa sighed. Dennis was extremely gorgeous; *he* certainly wasn't going to spend the summer feeling lonely.

Lisa's mother kept telling her that if there was anything real between them, Dennis would still be available when the summer was over. Lisa couldn't seem to explain to her that there had been only the *chance* for something—a chance she had very much wanted to see grow. Lisa had the feeling that even when her mother was a kid she had been old-fashioned. Maybe it was those romance novels she was always reading. True love seemed to have a better shot at surviving in those pages than it did in the real world.

"Hey, Lisa! Take your turn!"

Lisa blinked. "Sorry. Guess I was daydreaming."

"About that hunk we saw on the beach last Saturday?"

Lisa blushed. "No, not about some guy on the beach!"

"Well, I don't know why not," said Carrie impishly. "He was cute. I'll take him if you don't want him."

Lisa laughed in spite of herself. "Forget it. You're only ten!"

Carrie sighed. "I know. But I can dream, can't I?"

"Don't be so precocious. It's not healthy."

"Healthy? I don't even know what *precocious* means."

"Maybe we'd better drop Monopoly and switch to Scrabble. It wouldn't hurt you to get your nose inside a dictionary once in a while."

"Gag-a-mundo!"

"I take it back," said Lisa. "You're not precocious. You're warped." She smiled. "You're right about that guy, though. He *was* cute. Only he's a local. I don't think they like us summer people."

"Summer people, schmummer people. Boys like girls and girls like boys. He was looking back at you, you know."

Lisa felt herself blushing again. "Do you notice *everything?*" she asked in exasperation.

Carrie nodded. "Uh-huh. Even how red your face is getting."

"Twerp!" cried Lisa. She threw a potato chip at her sister.

Carrie threw one back. In a matter of seconds potato chips were flying back and forth across the Monopoly board and both girls were shrieking with laughter. When the potato chips were nearly gone, Lisa cleared Boardwalk and Park Place, and bounced a handful of little green houses off Carrie's forehead.

Carrie retaliated with a hotel from Marvin Gardens.

Even as the battle was escalating, Lisa knew it was a bad idea. But five days of sitting in the house and watching the rain streak the windows, five days of tiptoeing around so they wouldn't disturb their father, five days of playing endless rounds of Monopoly had left her like a tightened spring.

Just as the hilarity reached its peak, their father appeared at the door. "Lisa!" he barked. "Carrie!"

Carrie sprang to her feet, bumping the table as she did. Orange soda began pouring across the Monopoly game. Lisa quickly righted the bottle, but the game was already soaked.

"What is going on in here?" roared their father.

Suddenly their mother appeared behind him. Taking the situation in at a glance, she laid a gentle hand on her husband's arm. "Why don't you let me handle this, Martin? You go back to your work."

"Work? How can anyone work with all this racket? Would you two try to be a little more courteous? *And careful!*"

He turned and stormed away.

"I'm sorry, Mom," said Lisa. She was on the verge of tears. "I don't know what happened. We just got carried away."

"Hey, maybe we got Lisa'd away," said Carrie defensively.

"Carrie, be quiet," said her mother. "Look, get this mess cleaned up—and I mean cleaned up properly—and then we'll talk about it. I'll see you downstairs in a little while."

Lisa sighed. Her mother was angry. Well, she couldn't blame her for that. She and Carrie had acted pretty childish. But Lisa also got the feeling that her mother understood what had been behind the uproar. Maybe they wouldn't be in too much trouble.

She looked at her sister. "Let's get busy, twerplet."

Carrie fetched the paper towels. Lisa got some water.

They began mopping up.

Dr. Alice Miles was clearly unhappy. "I'm afraid this is all my fault. I just wanted everyone to have a good time here in the old place."

Lisa hated to see her grandmother upset. On the other hand, she had to agree with the old woman. It *was* her fault, since she was the one who had dragged them here. On the *other* other hand, Lisa knew that she herself had done little to improve the situation. For her grandmother's sake, she would have to try harder.

"Now, Mother," said Mrs. Burton, patting Dr. Miles's hand. "It was a perfectly lovely idea. Martin is just cranky because his writing isn't going well. And this weather has us all on edge." She paused. "Perhaps you and I should try to help the girls pass their time a little more wisely."

Lisa's mother looked at her pointedly. Lisa felt her stomach sink a little. Though her mother wasn't *terribly* angry, she certainly wasn't pleased with the two of them.

She turned her eyes away and looked out the window. The rain was still coming down.

It's not fair, she thought sullenly. *At least they all have some reason to want to be here—Daddy to work on his book; Gramma because she used to live here and she's on some memory trip; Mom and Carrie because it's more fun to be away in the summer than at home. And Smokey doesn't care where he is, as long as we feed him. If they don't like the rain, too bad. At least they wanted to be here. All I want is to be home with Dennis.*

"Perhaps we could take the girls to the movie over in Bridgeport," suggested her grandmother.

"We've seen it," said Lisa.

"Well, was it any good?"

"No."

"Oh," said Dr. Miles softly. Lisa felt guilty again.

"Now listen, girls," said Mrs. Burton sharply. "I know being stuck here in this weather hasn't been very pleasant. But it's not the end of the world. Nobody with any common sense and brains has any business being bored. There are all kinds of things you can do with your time. Read, write, draw—"

"For five straight days?" protested Carrie.

"All right, it *has* been a long time. We just have to make the best of it. Your father has waited six years for a chance to focus on this book. He's worked very hard to take care of us during that time. Now it's time we turned around and showed *him* a little consideration."

Lisa felt worse than ever. "You're right, Mom. We'll try. But we really didn't mean to cause trouble. Honest. It just sort of happened."

Her mother's face softened. "I know, honey. And I know how bored you are. But it seems strange. Your grandmother spent quite a few summers here with no television or stereo, and she survived."

"Well, what did you do, Gramma?" asked Lisa.

Dr. Miles looked surprised. "Oh, all sorts of things. Let's see. We did go to the movies a lot. Hmmm. That was only once a week, now that I think about it. That still left a lot of time open, didn't it?"

She didn't wait for an answer.

"What else? We listened to the radio, of course. And we talked to each other. I think we talked more in those days than people do now. And we used to play what they called parlor games. Monopoly was created sometime around then. But some of our games were more imaginative than that. We invented things. Used our minds."

Suddenly her face lit up.

"I remember one of my favorites. It wasn't a game, really. It was a kind of—well, it was just something you did. It was like a séance. Really very silly. We called it automatic writing."

"What's a séance?" asked Carrie.

"It's when people sit around and ask spirits to come and visit them," answered Lisa.

Carrie looked at her grandmother with new respect. "You used to do *that?*"

Dr. Miles laughed. "Well, we used to try. I was much younger then, and it was quite popular around here for a while."

"Let's try it."

Dr. Miles looked at her daughter. Mrs. Burton frowned slightly, then shrugged and said, "Oh, I don't see why not. Go ahead and set things up, Mother."

Dr. Miles smiled. "I think you'll enjoy this," she said enthusiastically. "Lisa, you pull down the shades. Carrie, help me move this end table. Judith, would you bring some chairs from the kitchen so we can sit around this little table?"

Lisa smiled. Despite the fact that her grandmother was older than most of the grandparents she knew ("Nearly eighty, and proud of it!" as she liked to say), Dr. Miles had always seemed young as grandmothers go. But now she was almost like a child in her excitement. She bustled about, arranging this, shifting that, as if everything had to be perfect for the "phenomenon" to take place—as if the spirits, or the mind, or whatever it was they were trying to call on, wouldn't cooperate if the place was a little out of order.

"There!" Dr. Miles stood back and surveyed the room with satisfaction. "That looks just fine. Now, let's all sit around the table. Who wants to go first? Lisa?"

Lisa shrugged. "Sure, I'll give it a try."

"Good. Carrie, you go turn off the lights."

Carrie ran to the switch beside the piano and turned

off the lights, which left the room surprisingly dark. Then she, Lisa, and Mrs. Burton took their places around the table while Dr. Miles got a candle.

"Well, at least it's not Monopoly," whispered Carrie. "I was so sick of passing Go I thought I would barf."

Lisa kicked her sister's ankle and hissed a quick *Shhh!* at her. She didn't want their grandmother feeling any worse than she already did.

Setting the candle in the center of the table, Dr. Miles looked directly at Carrie and said, "We must be very serious. Otherwise, it won't work. Lisa, put this in front of you." She handed Lisa a pad of writing paper. "Hold the pencil loosely."

Lisa did as she was told.

"Now close your eyes."

Again, Lisa did as she was told. In spite of herself, she began to feel a little tingly. There was something definitely eerie about doing all this in such an old house, on such a dark, dreary day.

"Carrie, Judith, join hands with me. Carrie and I will put our hands on Lisa's elbows, to close the circle."

Lisa felt the pressure of their fingertips at her elbows. She found it oddly reassuring.

"Now, you two also close your eyes. Close your eyes and concentrate."

For a moment there was silence. Then Dr. Miles said, "O spirits from the other side, if there are any here who wish to communicate with us, now is the time. Give us your message."

Lisa felt a shiver skitter down her spine. Then she heard Carrie trying to hold in a snort. She could almost sense her mother's look of disapproval. She wondered how she could do that with her eyes closed.

"Carrie," said Dr. Miles. "Please concentrate."

Lisa sat with her fingers loose, her hands resting on the pad. Suddenly she let out a little gasp. She had felt a terrible chill, as though a cold hand had been placed on her neck. Next she heard a loud knocking, like someone banging on the table.

She tried to open her eyes—and found that they were sealed shut!

The table began to vibrate.

It lurched forward.

Without her willing it to, Lisa's hand began to move.

2

Lisa tried to make her hand stop moving.

She couldn't.

"It's working!" Carrie whispered in awe. "Gramma, it's working!"

"Mother!" Lisa cried. "Make it stop!"

The table lurched again. Lisa felt faint—distant, as if she were far away from everything that was happening. From somewhere she heard her mother's voice calling her. The words sounded as if she were speaking through a pile of pillows. "Lisa! Lisa, open your eyes!"

Lisa tried to do as her mother told her. It was useless. She couldn't force the lids up. Somehow, she didn't care.

"Lisa!"

She sensed, with a detached sort of interest, that her hand was still rolling across the paper. Suddenly

15

another hand slammed down and closed over her wrist. For a moment there was a tremendous struggle as Lisa's hand tried to continue moving and the other hand, strong and sinewy, tried to make it stop.

"Lisa, open your eyes!"

It was her grandmother. Again, Lisa struggled to do as she was told. Suddenly she felt another moment of intense cold. She breathed out, and her eyes snapped open.

Her hand was lying limply on the table. Circling her wrist, still tightly clenched, were her grandmother's fingers. The pencil, now broken in half, lay on the paper.

Lisa looked around the table. The others' faces expressed varying degrees of shock and fear. Her mother was staring at her with nervous intensity. Carrie's face was glowing, her eyes shining with fascination at whatever it was that had just taken place. Then Lisa looked at her grandmother and caught her breath. Dr. Miles wore an expression that fell somewhere between longing and fear. But she was not looking at Lisa. Her eyes were focused on the paper beneath her hand.

Lisa looked down. Underneath her fingers was a set of intricate curlicues, tight and impossibly precise, more ornate than she could ever have made with her eyes open. They formed a frame around the edge of the paper.

In the center, in large, formal letters, was the message WELCOME HOME!

Lisa shivered. She knew *those* words had not come from her. They represented the last thing in the world she felt about this place.

Before she could speak, the lights came on. Almost immediately they went off again. It happened three times. Then there was a loud snap and the lights went out and stayed out. Dr. Miles tried the lamp standing next to her. It didn't work. "Obviously a farewell gesture from our visitor," she said, attempting a laugh.

"Visitor?" cried Lisa. "Gramma, what was going on here? Was I in contact with a spirit?"

"A ghost?" asked Carrie eagerly.

"Mother?" Mrs. Burton's voice was soft and worried.

Before Dr. Miles could speak, her son-in-law appeared on the stairwell. "What is going on down there?" he bellowed. "Carrie, have you been playing with the switches again?"

"It wasn't me!" Carrie cried, her voice full of indignation.

"I imagine it was the storm, Martin," Mrs. Burton said soothingly, her voice far calmer than Lisa would have thought possible under the circumstances.

As if to reinforce her point, lightning flickered outside, followed closely by a massive crash of thunder. Judith Burton smiled at her husband.

"Well, all that yelling wasn't caused by the storm," he said sharply. "Could you please keep it down? I can't concentrate with all this going on."

"I'm sorry, dear," said Mrs. Burton. "I think we'll go shopping—get out of your hair."

"The price of silence," said Mr. Burton, grumping as he always did when the subject of money came up. Lisa didn't take it too seriously; she had figured out long ago that it was a role he played. Muttering to himself, he stomped back up the stairs and headed for the room he was using for his office.

"Nice work, Mom," said Carrie.

"Hush!" said Mrs. Burton. "Lisa, are you all right?"

Lisa stopped to think. She hadn't had time to consider her condition since she had opened her eyes. "I guess so," she said. "A little shaky, maybe. What happened?"

"You tapped into the world beyond," said Carrie, trying—without much success—to make her high, piping voice sound spooky.

"Carrie," snapped Dr. Miles. "Don't be absurd."

"Well, how do *you* explain it?" asked Carrie.

Dr. Miles looked uncomfortable. "Well, there is a distinct possibility that Lisa was having a little joke at our expense—"

"I was not!" said Lisa indignantly.

Her grandmother raised her hands in a placating gesture. "I'm just trying to be scientific here, Lisa. The next most likely possibility is that your subconscious mind took over. That is the ultimate answer in most psychic phenomena. When you create the right mood, part of your brain—the part that dreams—can take control and do things you are not aware of. There's been quite a bit written about it."

Lisa felt a little tingle of fear. Not because of what her grandmother said, but because it was clear that the old woman was lying. Lisa could read it in her eyes, her voice, and she found it far scarier than what had just happened with the automatic writing.

What was her grandmother hiding?

"Okay, if the message came from Lisa's dream brain, then what did it mean?" asked Carrie.

"It was probably sarcastic, reflecting Lisa's unhappiness at being here," said Dr. Miles.

Lisa was about to object, but Dr. Miles placed her hand on Lisa's forearm. "Oh, come now. I know how you feel about all this, dear. And I'm terribly sorry. I was being selfish when I arranged it."

"No, Gramma. I—"

"Hush, child. Learn to accept an apology when it's offered."

"Well, it was fun, whatever it was," said Carrie eagerly. "Can I try next?"

"No!"

If Lisa had had any doubts that her grandmother was hiding something, they were dispelled by the tone in her voice when she answered Carrie.

"Why not?" asked Carrie.

"Because it was a bad idea in the first place," replied Dr. Miles. "I shouldn't have brought it up. I can remember seeing something like this once when I was a girl. I had forgotten about it until now. Some people are more sensitive to this kind of thing than others— the subconscious is closer to the surface in them, I guess."

"You mean Lisa has a weak mind?" asked Carrie gleefully.

"No! Now listen. It's possible to get swept up in this and think you're actually receiving messages from somewhere else. You're not. It's just a display of the power of the subconscious mind."

Mrs. Burton had been glancing back and forth from her mother to her daughter, as if she were trying to figure out what was going on. At Dr. Miles's last words she said firmly, "That makes sense. Let's put these things away."

Lisa and Carrie exchanged a glance. They both knew there was more going on than the grown-ups were willing to talk about. Lisa's subconscious might have provided that message, though she didn't think it was likely. But unless she had more powers than she was willing to believe, it sure hadn't made the table move!

She couldn't wait until she could get Carrie alone so they could compare notes.

Between the shopping trip and dinner, it was late that night before the two girls had a chance to talk.

"Tell me about what happened today," whispered Carrie when they had both climbed into the big old bed they had been forced to share.

Lisa didn't answer right away. The rain had stopped and their bedroom window was open. She lay on her side, watching a soft ocean breeze whisper over the sill and make the white curtain flutter in a ghostly way. Finally she said, "It's hard to say; it was as if I wasn't there—like I had stepped into another room or something."

"Do you think the message was from a ghost trying to communicate with us?" asked Carrie eagerly.

Lisa shivered. "I hope not. I like Gramma's explanation better."

"You know that wasn't true!" said Carrie fiercely. *"She* sure didn't believe it."

"I know," said Lisa. "That's what really scared me."

"Me, too! But not as much as when the table moved. You should have seen Mom's face when that happened! That was when I knew something was weird. There was nothing to make the table move like that. Nothing at all." Carrie paused, then whispered, "Want to try it again?"

"Are you crazy? Carrie, for all we know, this place really is haunted. I mean, it's old enough. All kinds of things might have happened here. You want to stir things up any more than we already have?"

"Sure! It would give us something to tell the kids back home! Lisa, this place is so boring I could barf. At least a ghost would be interesting."

"You say that now. I'd like to be there the first time you actually see one."

"I'll just ... just ..."

Carrie's voice faltered and her eyes grew wide. Lisa turned in the direction her sister was staring and gave a tiny gasp of fear.

A woman had just stepped through the door. Not through the doorway. Through the *door!* She came gliding through the solid wood as though it were mist.

Both girls slid up against the back of the bed. Lisa felt a cold chill shiver down her spine. The woman seemed to be made of light, a soft blue glow you could see right through. She was dressed in old-fashioned clothes. Her long hair flowed down her back. Though it was difficult to make out the details of her face, something about her was oddly familiar.

Carrie's hand crept along under the sheet and took Lisa's. Lisa squeezed it, not daring to make any other move.

"I'm scared!" whispered Carrie, huddling against her.

Before Lisa could answer, the figure began floating toward the bed.

Lisa put her arm around Carrie, holding her protectively.

The woman moved slowly in their direction, looking at them intently, as if she were having a hard time getting them in focus.

The room had become very cold.

21

The woman stopped at the foot of the bed.

"What do you want?" cried Lisa.

The woman made no answer. The terrible cold grew deeper.

Lisa swallowed. The woman continued to stare at them.

No. Not *them*.

She was staring at Carrie.

Then Lisa caught a sense of the woman's emotions. She shivered. It was almost as if she were a radio receiver, tuned in to what the woman was feeling. Suddenly she wanted to cry. The woman was radiating such strong love and sorrow that Lisa thought her own heart must break.

The woman smiled and reached out to Carrie.

"Welcome home," she whispered.

Then she vanished.

3

For a moment the two girls sat in stunned silence. There had been no aura of menace about the ghost. Yet what they had seen was terrifying. Part of what made it so frightening was the sense of having been at the edge of a great mystery, the feeling that they had been allowed a tiny peek at an awesome secret.

"Should we go get Mom and Dad?" whispered Carrie at last.

"I'm not sure," said Lisa. It was strange: She knew that if she had been alone when the ghost arrived, her scream would have woken the dead—any that weren't already up and wandering. But having someone else with you—even someone younger, like Carrie—made something like this much easier to deal with. As to rousing their parents—well, her father was far too practical and scientific for this kind of . . . "nonsense."

She smiled. She could practically hear him saying the word.

Their mother *might* believe them. But even if she did, what could she do about it? It wasn't as if you could go to the store and get a can of spray-on ghost repellent. The only thing she could try to do would be to convince their father to take them home. But he wasn't apt to do that on the basis of a ghost story.

And it was equally likely that she might suspect the whole story was just a pretense to try to put an early end to the trip.

"I think we should keep this to ourselves," said Lisa at last.

"Sacred sister pact?" asked Carrie.

Lisa nodded. "Our personal secret, until our dying day. Because it's the most awesome thing that's ever happened to either of us."

Carrie held out her hand in the private gesture they had created the year before, and they shook on it. Then they huddled together and stayed awake long into the night, talking in hushed voices as they waited to see if the ghost would reappear.

But she did not show herself again, and eventually both girls drifted into a deep sleep.

When Lisa yawned and stirred the next morning, she had the feeling that something was different. It took her a moment to realize what had changed. The sun was shining!

She couldn't believe it. After five days of constant rain, she had begun to feel that it was natural that the first thing you would hear when you woke was rain pattering against the windows, drumming on the roof, and pouring from the eaves. But this morning there were actually a few birds singing in the yard. All at once everything seemed a little more bearable . . . even the strange events of the previous night.

She slipped from beneath the covers and went to poke her head out the window. The sun was bright on the tangled, overgrown garden. Even the sight of the ruined summerhouse with its collapsed roof and broken walls couldn't bring down her mood—though she hated it when beautiful old things were allowed to get run-down like that.

She glanced up. The sky was gloriously clear, not a cloud in sight. She pulled her head back inside, then turned and hurried down the hall to take her shower. She planned to be out on the beach early. If nothing else, she would like to have a tan to show for her summer exile.

She wondered what Dennis was doing. Sleeping, probably. Morning was not his favorite time of the day.

When Lisa returned to the room after her shower, Carrie was sitting up in bed, looking nervous. "There you are," she said, breathing a sigh of relief. "I was beginning to get worried."

"For heaven's sake," said Lisa, toweling her hair. "How far away did you think I could get in—" She stopped. The haunted look in her sister's eyes made her stomach turn. "I'm sorry, Carrie. I shouldn't have left you alone!"

"It's all right," Carrie replied quickly. "Really. It's just that last night was . . ."

"Weird," said Lisa, finishing the sentence. "Absolutely. I was thinking about it all through my shower. So what do you think? I know we swore as sacred sisters. But maybe we should tell Mom and Dad what happened anyway...."

"Are you kidding? They'd call in a whole army of shrinks."

Lisa grimaced. "That was what I decided, too. And I'm in no mood to be analyzed." She glanced at the window. It was weird how a bright, sunny day made it hard to hold on to the reality of last night's strangeness. Turning back to Carrie, she said, "How do you feel? Are you all right?"

"Sure. It was just a little welcoming party, right? Or maybe it was that pizza we had for dinner. Can two people have the same nightmare?"

Lisa smiled. "No, but they can both have the same breakfast. Come on, let's go get something to eat."

Their mother was standing in the kitchen when they came downstairs. "Good morning, girls! Did you sleep well?"

"*I* didn't," Carrie said. "Didn't you hear Lisa snoring?"

Lisa didn't know whether to smile or frown. Carrie was certainly acting like her old self. Maybe she hadn't been too scared after all. Turning to her mother, she said, "I'm going to the beach today. Okay?"

"Of course," said Mrs. Burton. "It's about time you had a chance to get some sunshine."

"I'll come, too!" said Carrie quickly. Lisa sighed. She really didn't want her sister along. But it wasn't a good day to leave her alone.

Though they got to the beach by ten o'clock, it was already crowded. *Looks like* everyone *wants to wel-*

come back the sunshine, thought Lisa as she scanned the broad stretch of sand for a vacant spot.

"Over there!" said Carrie.

"Good eyes, twerp." They made their way to the spot and spread out their blanket. Lisa slipped out of her shirt. As she rummaged in her beach bag for the tanning lotion, Carrie examined her critically, then said, "You're not in bad shape for your age."

"What's that supposed to mean?"

"Well, let's just say that if that guy comes along again today, you shouldn't have any trouble attracting his attention. Of course, that bathing suit doesn't hurt. Did I tell you how mad Daddy was when he saw it? I heard him complaining to Mom the week you got it."

Lisa looked down and assessed herself. The red bathing suit was a little skimpy, she supposed. But no more so than those that the other girls were wearing. Of course, she knew her father's answer to that particular point: "And if most girls were eating toad sandwiches, would you want one, too?"

"Stop being so hormonal and put some lotion on my back," she said to Carrie. "I want to get a start on my tan."

"All right, all right. Just give me a minute, will you?"

As Carrie began to arrange her things on her towel, Lisa stretched out on her back and closed her eyes. The sun against her skin was warm and soothing, the sound of the waves a few yards away gentle, rhythmic, and wonderfully relaxing. Lisa thought she might go back to sleep and catch up on some of the rest she had lost the night before.

"Okay," said Carrie, "give me the bottle."

Lisa opened her eyes, then smiled. For Carrie, going

27

to the beach was a major expedition. After spreading her towel neatly across the sand, she had pinned it down at the corners with carefully selected items from her beach bag. At the top was her Walkman. Next to the Walkman was a pile of comic books. And next to them were the teen fan magazines that Carried loved. Running down the side of the towel was a revolting array of Twinkies, Ding Dongs, and Fritos. Kneeling in the middle of all this was Carrie, wearing a bright yellow two-piece bathing suit, which did nothing for her. She had sunglasses perched on her snub of a nose.

"If you want me to do your back, you'll have to roll over," she said.

Lisa lay on her stomach and luxuriated in the feel of the sun on her shoulders. "Yow!" she cried when the cold lotion hit her skin. But it warmed up quickly, and felt good.

"Uh-oh," said Carrie. "Don't look now. But there he is!"

"Who?"

"The hunk!"

"Carrie, shut up," said Lisa, lifting her head to see who Carrie was talking about.

It was the boy she had spotted the week before. Lisa blushed. He was walking toward them!

"Carrie! Did you do something to attract his attention?" She had a horrified thought. "Did you wink at him?"

"I'm not that stupid," whispered Carrie. "Chill out. Maybe you just got lucky."

The boy stopped in front of them. "Lisa?" he asked.

She scrambled to her feet, suddenly feeling uncovered. She wished she had picked a bathing suit that wasn't quite so tiny after all! Nervously she ran her hand through her curly, dark brown hair.

"Your mother told me I'd find you here," said the boy.

Lisa gave him a puzzled look. "I've heard a lot of lines before, but ..."

He laughed, and Lisa found herself smiling, too. His laugh was deep and rich, not at all forced.

Everything else about him was attractive, too. His thick hair, long and parted in the middle, had been bleached by the sun to the color of light straw. He had impish blue eyes and a full mouth. He was lean, yet his faded cotton shirt had to stretch across his broad shoulders.

"Actually, I did stop to talk to you about a pickup," he said. "But you're the one who has to do it. Your mother wants you to get these things on your way home." He pulled a piece of paper from his shirt pocket. "She sent this to pay for them," he added, handing her a twenty-dollar bill.

"Why did she send this with you?" asked Lisa, trying to get her bearings.

"My dad and I are doing some work at the place you rented. The owners sent us. When we got there this morning, we realized we needed some more tools. Dad sent me back to get them, and your mother asked if I would be going by the beach on the way. I lied and told her yes."

"That was pretty forward of you," said Lisa. But the smile on her face made it clear she was delighted he had taken the liberty.

"It seemed like a good way to get to meet you," he said. "My name is Brian. Brian Holme. I'm one of the local yokels."

"And I'm one of the invaders," said Lisa. "This is my sister, Carrie."

"Hi," said Carrie. "I think I'll go get an ice-cream cone."

Lisa didn't know whether to thank her sister or strangle her. It was nice of her to get out of the way, but did she have to be so obvious?

"It's nice to meet you," said Brian to Carrie. "Maybe we can talk again some time."

Carrie laughed and ran down the beach.

"Cute kid," said Brian.

"She's okay most of the time." Lisa sat back down on her towel. "So what are you doing at the house?"

"We're working on some of the windows. The wood's rotting around them. As a matter of fact, I have to get going. Dad's going to wonder where I am. See you later!"

With that he was gone. Lisa frowned. Had she said something wrong?

She stretched out in the sunshine and scowled at the rolling water of the Atlantic. Maybe Carrie had scared him off. *Well, it's no big deal,* she told herself. *He's only a boy.* She sighed. If only he wasn't so darn cute!

It was shortly after two when Lisa and Carrie arrived back at the house with the groceries their mother had requested. Lisa was delighted to see Brian standing on a ladder that was leaning against the west wall.

"Hi!" he called when he spotted her. "How was the beach?"

"Super! How are the windows?"

He made a face. "They're a real pane!"

Lisa groaned.

"Sill and all," he continued, "this is a high-glass job."

"Stop!" she cried. "I think I'm going to be sick. Do you always make such rotten puns?"

"Only when I'm standing where no one can get at me." He paused. "Are you going to be around for a while?" he asked, his voice suddenly serious.

"I think so. Why?"

"I just wanted to talk to you for a few minutes before I go. Okay?"

"Sure!"

Lisa hummed happily to herself as she unpacked her curling iron. An honest-to-goodness date! Suddenly the summer seemed much more interesting. Even the old house didn't bother her the way it had.

Carrie sat on the bed, watching her get ready to go. "Do you think you'll be out late?" she asked in a worried voice.

"Not too late. Why?"

Before Carrie could answer, Lisa realized what was on her mind. "Oh, Carrie! I'm sorry!"

Carrie shrugged. "I'll be all right," she said in a martyred tone.

Lisa cursed herself and her sister and the stupid house. Everything seemed very complicated. For a moment she thought she would rather go back to being bored.

"Look, Mom and Dad won't be here, either. But you can probably get Gramma to let you stay up late. Tell her there's an old movie you want to watch. The two of you and Smokey can keep yourselves company. I doubt the ghost will appear again, anyway. I mean, we've been here for two weeks already. It's not like this has been going on every night."

"I know," said Carrie. "Look, don't worry about it."

Lisa frowned. She knew that was exactly what she would be doing. All night.

"Well, don't you look nice," said her grandmother as Lisa came down the stairs. "That white dress is so ... summery. It sets off your dark curls perfectly."

Lisa smiled. Her grandmother would probably find something nice to say if she came downstairs in a burlap sack.

"Where are you going tonight?"

"To the movie over in Bridgeport."

Dr. Miles raised an eyebrow. "Oh?" she said with a twinkle in her eye. "I thought it wasn't any good."

Lisa blushed. "Well, maybe I misjudged it. You never know!"

Her grandmother laughed. "Have a good time, dear." She kissed her on the cheek. "I won't wait up for you. And your parents probably won't get home until after you do. Your mother has cabin fever, too. She's going to make the most of her evening out."

Lisa's reply was cut short by a knock at the door.

"That must be Brian!" cried Carrie. "I'll get it!"

Lisa sighed. Why did Carrie always have to be so eager?

Lisa sat glumly beside Brian as they drove back from the film.

"What's the matter?" he asked.

"Nothing!" she said, lying and flashing him a quick smile.

32

Which was part of the problem. Everything was fine; *too* fine. It had been a wonderful evening, and now Lisa didn't want it to end—partly because she had the feeling he would never ask her out again. The beach was filled with summer girls, and Brian could have his choice. Most of them were more sophisticated than she was, prettier, more interesting.

Suddenly she felt very inadequate.

"Didn't you like the movie?" he asked.

"It was wonderful!" she cried.

Brian looked at her and made a face.

Lisa burst out laughing. The picture had been terrible, and they both knew it.

"You shouldn't lie like that," said Brian, smiling. "It damages your credibility."

"My mother calls that a 'little white.' According to her, little whites are 'a necessary social evil.'"

"What is she?" asked Brian. "A preacher?"

Lisa smiled. "You might say that. Her sermons are all delivered in my bedroom, though. To an audience of one. Me."

Brian laughed. "My mother's a preacher, too. Her favorite topic is how I should settle down and stop dating so many girls."

"So, you're a real heartbreaker, huh?" She tried to sound casual, but it didn't quite work. Her stomach was in knots.

Brian frowned. "I hope not. I just want to have a good time. Seeing one person all the time can get boring, don't you think?"

Lisa frowned, certain he was telling her he didn't want to go out again. And she was sure it was because he knew he could find more interesting people on the beach, any day, any time. She had paid attention to

33

the competition when she was working on her tan. Most of the girls summering on the island were from wealthy families. A lot of them went to private schools and took lessons of some sort—everything from horseback riding to karate. She could see why Brian wouldn't want to bother with her. She was boring, boring, boring! She wished desperately she could think of something to make herself more interesting.

"Do you believe in spirits?" she asked suddenly.

"What?"

"You know: ghosts, spooks, voices from beyond?"

Brian paused. When he answered, Lisa was surprised at how serious his voice sounded. "I'm not sure," he said slowly. "I plan on becoming a scientist—marine biology. I know I should be very rational. But, yeah, I guess I sort of do. The idea of a spirit world has always fascinated me."

Lisa felt a surge of elation. "Well, did you ever try something called automatic writing?"

Brian shook his head. "I've heard of it. But I never tried it. Why?"

"Oh, we were fooling around with it yesterday," she said casually. "My grandmother was teaching us how to do it."

"Did you have any luck?"

"Believe it or not, we did. I got a message from somewhere. And . . ." Her voice trailed off. She wasn't sure how much she wanted to say about the table knocking or the other things that had happened.

"What did it say?" asked Brian, a note of intense interest in his voice.

" 'Welcome home.' "

"That's weird. What do you suppose it meant?"

"I don't know. I got scared, and we stopped the séance."

"Do you want to try it again tonight?" asked Brian.

"Oh, no, I—" She stopped. His voice was so eager. He really was interested. "Sure," she said. "Why not?"

They were just pulling into the driveway.

"It doesn't bother you to do something like that in this house?" he asked.

Lisa looked at him curiously. "Why should it?"

"Well, the place has quite a reputation."

Lisa felt the hair on the back of her neck begin to stand up. "What do you mean?"

Brian looked at her in surprise. "You didn't know? You're staying in the most haunted place on Sayers Island!"

4

Lisa's skin began to prickle. Looking at Brian intently, she said softly, almost angrily, "What do you mean?"

"Hey, don't get mad at me! I'm just telling you what people say. I don't know if the place is really haunted. But it does have that reputation." He paused, then added, "You mean you really didn't know?"

"No." Lisa glanced at the house. "But I could have guessed."

She wondered briefly why her grandmother hadn't said anything, then realized at once that the answer was simple: Dr. Alice Miles was far too scientific to believe in ghosts.

"Reality may be weirder than you think, Gramma," she muttered.

"What did you say?" asked Brian.

Lisa blushed. "Nothing." She turned to him. "Do you still want to come in?"

"Sure. It's only quarter of eleven. I've got plenty of time before I turn into a pumpkin. Besides, we can't very well have a séance in the car."

Lisa forced a small laugh. She was sorry now that she had raised the idea of a séance. There was no sense in stirring things up any further. But she couldn't think of a way out, at least not without looking totally dweebish.

A shot rang out as they entered the kitchen.

"Carrie!" yelled Lisa automatically. "Turn down the TV!"

Instantly Carrie's face appeared around the edge of the door. "You're back!"

"No, we're still someplace else. This is just a mirage."

"Hey, give her a break," said Brian gently. "Hi, Carrie. How are you?"

Carrie shrugged. "Okay, I guess. It's been kind of dead around here. Gramma went to bed a half hour ago, and this television program is so stupid I could puke. I wish this place got cable."

"Why don't you just turn it off and read a book?" suggested Lisa.

Carrie stuck a finger in her mouth and made a gagging gesture.

Lisa turned to Brian. "See what I have to live with?"

He smiled. "I have *four* younger sisters."

"Oh, you poor boy!" cried Lisa. "Here, have a seat. You need to conserve your energy."

Brian laughed and took a place at the kitchen table.

"We're going to have a séance, Carrie. Do you want to join us?"

Carrie looked at Lisa nervously. "What are you going to do that for?"

Brian shrugged. "Lisa was telling me you had some luck with it yesterday. I just want to see how you do it."

Carrie hesitated, and Lisa almost suggested they forget it. But she was afraid she'd never see Brian again if she did.

"Sure," said Carrie at last. "I'll get the stuff."

"What stuff?"

"Oh, paper and pencils," said Lisa as Carrie left the room. "Can't do automatic writing without them, you know."

"Here we go," said Carrie, trotting back into the kitchen a moment later. She carried a pad of paper, a handful of pencils, and a candle in a holder. "I figured we could use this when we dim the lights," she said, lifting the candle.

Lisa looked at her little sister with respect. Whatever fear she had felt she had overcome pretty quickly.

"So what do we do?" asked Brian.

"First light the candle," said Carrie, taking charge. "Then we'll take our places around the table." She was standing by the door, waiting to hit the light switch. As soon as Brian had lit the candle, she darkened the room. "Now, you have to be very serious," she said as she returned and took a seat. "Otherwise it won't work."

Brian gave Lisa a wink. He was obviously enjoying Carrie's businesslike manner.

"All right, who wants to go first?" Carrie asked.

"I do," said Brian. "I'm not sure I trust the two of you not to pull some stunt on me. Maybe tell one of those 'socially necessary little whites.' " He smiled at Lisa, and she felt her cheeks flush.

"Okay," said Carrie. "Here, put this in front of you." She handed him the pad. "Now, pick up the pencil and hold it as if you were ready to write. Then just relax."

Brian did as Carrie instructed. Though he kept a perfectly straight face, there was a merry look in his eye. Lisa found it very attractive, even in these uncomfortable circumstances.

"Now, you have to close your eyes," said Carrie. "Lisa and I are going to hold hands. Then each of us will put a hand on your elbow to complete the circle. All right?"

Brian nodded.

Lisa looked at Carrie across the table. The flickering candle made the shadows on her childish face shift and change. Her eyes were shining with excitement.

Lisa glanced around the kitchen. With nothing but candlelight to break the gloom, it suddenly seemed very spooky. She told herself it was simply because the place was so old-fashioned. The cupboard, the big stove, the door to the cellar—each of them was out of date enough to give the place a feeling of age that she found unnerving in this situation.

"Close your eyes," said Carrie. *"Concentrate!"*

Lisa did as she was directed, giving Brian's elbow a little squeeze.

Carrie began to speak. "O spirits from the other side, if there are any here who wish to communicate with us, now is the time. Give us your message!"

Lisa was impressed. As near as she could tell, those were the exact words her grandmother had used.

They sat in silence for a moment. Suddenly Lisa felt a cold draft on her neck. She shivered and tightened her hand on Brian's elbow.

Now she began to hear something. It started so softly she was hardly aware it was there. Slowly it grew louder, more distinct. It was the voice of a woman, weeping softly, yet sounding as if her heart would break.

Lisa opened her eyes and looked around. The voice seemed to come from somewhere above them. Carrie's eyes were pinched shut. Brian's face showed nothing but intense concentration.

Couldn't they hear it?

"Carrie!" she whispered.

"Shhh!"

Lisa shuddered. They *didn't*; they didn't hear it at all.

And it was still getting louder!

Suddenly the cupboard door behind her swung open, then slammed shut. With a yowl, Smokey dashed out of the room. Carrie's eyes flew open. She was about to say something when the table lurched and Brian's hand began to move across the paper.

The candle flickered wildly, and the cupboard doors began to slam. Starting at the far end of the wall and moving down the length of the kitchen, each of them flew open and then banged shut.

Lisa gasped. The candlestick had started to float! Heart pounding, she watched it rise until it was hovering about a foot above the table.

She became aware of Brian's hand, scratching across the paper. She looked at the pad, trying to read the words, and choked back a cry of fright. On the first line was a series of exclamation points. Printed in bold letters on the next line was a single word: DANGER!

As she watched, Brian printed the word again. DANGER! Then he added: LEAVE THIS PLACE AT ONCE!

Behind Lisa the last cupboard door was slamming back and forth. Suddenly the flame on the candle shot up, roaring to several times its normal height, almost like a blowtorch. The voice of the sobbing woman changed, the sorrow replaced by anger. As the woman let out a horrible scream of rage, Lisa pulled back from the table, breaking her contact with Brian and Carrie.

The flapping cupboard door slammed shut so hard it rattled all the dishes on the shelves. The candle flew across the room and smashed against the wall above the kitchen sink, spattering wax in all directions. The pencil in Brian's hand burst apart, disintegrating in a fury of splinters.

Brian's eyes flew open. He looked at Carrie and Lisa as if he were on the verge of a heart attack. In a voice that sounded like rustling corn husks, he whispered, "What in God's name is going on here?"

The same words were shouted almost simultaneously by an older, sharper voice. Dr. Miles came rushing into the room, her robe flapping, her long white hair flying behind her. For a moment Lisa thought her grandmother looked like a ghost herself.

Brian clearly thought so, too. He started back from the table, then relaxed just a hair as he realized who it was.

"We were doing automatic writing, Gramma," said Carrie, her voice soft, scared.

Dr. Miles's eyes widened, and she was clearly furious. Turning to Brian, she said—quite politely but in

41

a voice sharp as a knife's edge—"I think you had better pick yourself up and head for home."

That made Lisa feel awful; Brian was clearly shaken by what had happened. It didn't seem fair to send him out into the night all alone.

Dr. Miles seemed to sense the same thing, for she immediately relented and asked him to stay for a little while. "You can help us clean the place up," she said tartly. "Something I would like to have done before Lisa and Carrie's parents get home."

There wasn't that much to clean up, really. Two or three dishes had slipped out of the cupboards and shattered on the floor. There were splinters from the pencil, and wax where the candle had struck the wall. The wax was the only real problem. It had left grease spots on the wallpaper that wouldn't come out, no matter what they did.

"Leave it," said Dr. Miles finally. "Sit down. I want to talk to you. All three of you."

When they had gathered at the table, Dr. Miles glanced up at the wax stain and said, "It almost blends into the wallpaper anyway. One of the virtues of having a busy pattern."

Lisa felt the tension begin to ease a little. But if her grandmother was less angry, she was no less serious. "I'm not going to say this again," she said sternly. "So pay attention. What you did tonight was foolish. I would be angrier, but it's my own fault this all began. I doubt I have ever done anything more mindless than teaching you girls about automatic writing yesterday. But I was desperate for something to distract you, and I didn't really think things out."

She paused and looked each of them in the eye. "You're young. You may not want to be reminded of that fact, but it's true—sometimes painfully so, to someone of my age. Now, automatic writing can be fun. But it can also be dangerous, especially for young people. Poltergeist activity like you saw here tonight, rare as it is, usually occurs in households where there are teenagers. Your minds are still developing. The subconscious is in chaos. Automatic writing is a way to tap that subconscious. But it's uncontrolled."

She stared at Lisa. Lowering her voice, she said intensely, almost urgently, "The mind has powers we don't yet understand. You can do yourselves great damage. Please, use some common sense. Let's not stir anything up again. All right?"

They all nodded their assent.

Dr. Miles smiled. "Good. Now, I'd just as soon your parents didn't know about this. So if you're willing, we'll keep it to ourselves for the time being."

Lisa blinked in surprise. It wasn't usual, at least in her experience, for grown-ups to hide things from one another. But she respected her grandmother, and was willing to do as she asked, despite how odd it seemed.

A few minutes later Brian got up to go. He still looked somewhat shaky, and Dr. Miles wouldn't let him leave until he had assured her that he felt solid enough to drive home.

Lisa wondered if she would ever see him again.

Lisa opened her eyes. The bedroom was dark. It was still the middle of the night.

What had woken her?

She lay still, listening, then shivered. It was that woman. She was crying again.

Where was her voice coming from?

43

Lisa glanced over at Carrie, who was sleeping peacefully next to her. No point in waking her.

Lisa lay still, listening, and thinking. She wanted to go back to sleep herself. But she couldn't, not with that woman's sorrow penetrating her the way it did.

Finally she slipped from between the sheets. Trying not to wake Carrie, she groped in the dark for her robe and slippers. She had a book of matches in her robe pocket, for the candle that rested on the table next to the bed. (One of the quaint touches her mother had added to the house.) She lit the candle and watched it sputter for a moment before settling into a clear, steady flame.

"All right," she whispered. "Let's see if we can find out what's bothering you—whoever you are."

She crept into the hallway. Holding her robe closed with one hand, she lifted the candle with the other, so that it cast its light in a wider circle. She looked in both directions. Nothing in the hallway.

She was frightened, of course. But it was not an overwhelming fear. And the fact that she was going to look for the voice gave her a sense of control that made her feel safer.

She tiptoed along the passage, the thick carpet almost completely muffling the sound of her movements. She stopped at the other two bedrooms, listening intently for the crying. It did not come from behind either of those doors. Not that she had expected it to. But she had figured she should make sure.

Several times she considered turning back. But the crying was so haunting, so compelling, that she couldn't. It was clear that something was desperately wrong. Lisa felt the woman's sorrow, felt a great compassion for the pain that caused her to weep so deeply. Somehow she had to help.

Her father often referred to her as "the bleeding heart of the Burton family." He said it jokingly, but she knew he took a certain amount of pride in her compassion.

It was compassion that drove her on now, compassion stronger than fear that propelled her along the empty hallway in search of the sobbing woman.

When Lisa reached the end of the hall, she stopped at the stairway that led to the first floor. Holding the candle before her, she stood, motionless, trying to see what was down the stairs. It was no use. Yet it seemed that the sobbing was definitely louder in that direction.

Lisa tiptoed down the stairs, trying to move as quietly as a spirit herself. The candle shook in her trembling hand.

The woman was on the couch in the living room. She had flung herself down so that her face was buried in the cushions. Her shoulders were shaking.

Lisa could see the couch right through the woman's body.

Hesitantly she took another step forward.

The sobbing stopped, as if the woman had become aware of Lisa's presence. For a moment she remained perfectly still.

Then she turned and looked at Lisa.

It was the same woman who had walked through their bedroom door the night before. Her hand flew to her mouth, as if she was terrified at seeing Lisa.

Without a word, she vanished.

Lisa stood for a moment. Then, feeling oddly disconsolate, as if the woman's sorrow had transferred itself to her, she turned and trudged back up the stairs.

45

5

Brian's mouth was set in a firm line. "You've got to get out of there."

Nearby three children shrieked with laughter as they chased a beach ball being propelled by a sudden breeze.

"How?" asked Lisa, for the third time. She was starting to feel exasperated by Brian's insistence.

"I don't know! I have a hard enough time getting my *own* parents to do anything. But you can't stay. It's too dangerous!"

Lisa patted his hand. He drew it back, and she gave herself a mental kick for acting as if she were trying to calm an upset child. The conversation was not going well at all. "Do you want to go in the water?" she asked, nodding toward the sparkling surf.

"Don't try to change the subject!"

She sighed. "Look, Brian. My father is a scientist. He doesn't believe in spooks and spirits. He wouldn't believe in one if it climbed into his lap and ruffled his hair while he was working. My grandmother's a scientist, too. I mean, she's retired from teaching, but her mind still works like a scientist's. Even if she thought this stuff really was dangerous, she'd probably rather stay and study it than run away. Besides, that house was her home every summer as a child. She just isn't going to believe anything really dangerous is going on."

"Do you?" asked Brian.

A group of men jogged by, huffing and panting. Lisa turned to watch them, squinting her eyes against the bright sunshine. The ocean was calm, the circling gulls quiet. Her radio, set low, was playing "The Corridors of My Mind."

It seemed an odd time and place to be talking about ghosts.

"No," she said at last. "There is *something* going on. But I don't think it's dangerous."

"What about that message?"

A worried look crossed her face. "I don't know. I'll admit it was strange. But even stranger things are happening." She turned and peered into his blue eyes. They looked as troubled as she felt. "Promise you won't think I'm weird?"

"I think you're weird already. I doubt you can tell me anything that will make it worse."

Lisa frowned.

"I'm sorry," he said quickly. "I shouldn't have said that. Tell me what you started to say."

"I've seen the ghost."

Brian stared at her.

"Twice," she continued. "And I just don't think there's anything harmful about her."

Speaking quickly, she told Brian about her two encounters with the spirit. "She's very sad," she concluded. "Sad, but not dangerous. In fact, I think she needs help."

Brian snorted. "What are you planning to be when you grow up? A shrink for the walking dead?"

"No, a veterinarian. But that doesn't mean I can't try to help someone who's in trouble."

"Right!" exclaimed Brian. "Which is exactly what *I'm* trying to do right now. You're in trouble, and I'm trying to help. *Get out of that house!*"

Lisa stood and brushed the sand from her legs. "This conversation is going nowhere. I'll see you later." She grabbed her beach bag and started to stalk away.

"Lisa!"

She paused, then turned back.

"I'm sorry. We won't talk about it anymore." He patted the blanket. "Stay. Please?"

She smiled. "I'm not going to make you work to convince me." She dropped the bag in the sand and sat back down beside him.

Shortly after supper that evening Lisa went to the room she shared with Carrie and sat at the desk. She hesitated for a moment, then took out several sheets of paper and a pencil.

She bit her lip. This was stupid. Her grandmother had told her not to do it. Brian was pleading with her to get her family out of the house altogether. And here she was, trying to make contact with the ghost again.

Somehow, being forbidden to do the automatic writing only made her want to do it more. And the more she tried not to think about it, the more her mind turned in that direction. It was like being on a diet and trying to ignore the last cookie in the cookie jar.

And her curiosity was driving her wild. Why did the spirit stare at Carrie? What did the words *Welcome home* mean? And why was the ghost weeping in the night? Lisa felt as though she would explode if she couldn't find the answers to these questions.

She had gone to the library after leaving the beach. It closed early on Saturday, and she had just barely made it. But she had found a small book on spiritualism that had a whole chapter on automatic writing. One of the points it made was that the activity didn't require a group; one person alone could try to induce a trance.

Lisa got up and closed the bedroom door, hoping Carrie wouldn't barge in. She didn't want anyone to see what she was doing. She frowned. Really, she only wanted to help the weeping woman. But she felt vaguely . . . dirty. It was the deception, she decided. She had told her grandmother she wouldn't do this anymore.

She drew the shade against the twilight. Somehow it seemed to make sense to darken the room.

She returned to the desk, picked up her pencil, and closed her eyes.

"What next?" she asked herself. She tried to recall the instructions in the book.

"Make your mind a blank" was one of the things it had said. She tried to put everything out of her head. It was amazingly difficult. Her brain seemed rebellious, unwilling to think about *nothing*. As soon as she thought she had her mind clear, a stray thought would come wandering through, seemingly from nowhere. If she tried to ignore it, it would practically jump up and down shouting for attention. And as soon as she did give it any attention her mind was off and wandering, so that a few minutes later she would realize with a start that she had been completely distracted from what she was trying to do.

"O spirit from the other side," she whispered. "If you wish to communicate, now is the time. Give me your message."

Nothing happened. She waited, trying to empty her brain, to make space for the spirit to work through her.

"Spirit from the other side," she whispered again. "Give me your message." She realized her tone had become almost demanding.

"You'll never contact the other world that way," she muttered. "Calm down, Burton, before you scare her away."

She found the idea somewhat amusing—that the ghost might be scared of her, instead of vice versa. She began to imagine herself face to face with the spirit, standing up to it with fearless ease.

She smiled at the imaginary picture.

It wasn't until a moment later that she realized her hand was moving.

Lisa looked at the paper in disgust. It was covered with a series of looping scrawls. If any message was hidden there, it was beyond her comprehension. The whole thing looked as if it had been done by a baby, or maybe a crazy person. She wadded the paper into a ball and tossed it in the wastebasket.

She hesitated, then placed her hand on the next sheet of paper. She closed her eyes and began to concentrate on emptying her mind. It was a little easier this time, but her hand lay still and unmoving.

Suddenly Lisa shivered.

Someone else was in the room. She could sense the presence as surely as if it had been announced with a trumpet fanfare.

Yet everything was silent.

She looked around uneasily. "Where are you?" she asked, her voice quavering.

No answer.

Lisa jumped. A drop of water had fallen on her wrist. She looked at it as if water were something she had never seen before.

It was followed by another drop, then another.

She looked up. The water was dripping from the ceiling.

She jumped out of her chair and pulled up the shade.

The sky was clear. And in five days of rain the ceiling had not leaked once.

So where was the water coming from?

Lisa looked around the room again. "What does it mean?" she whispered. "Why is this happening?"

No one answered.

But the ceiling continued to drip.

And somewhere in the distance Lisa heard the sound of a woman weeping.

"Lisa, it's for you!"

Lisa came to with a start. She had been listening to the weeping woman and must have fallen into a sort of trance. She was slightly shocked to realize she was sitting at her desk. The last she remembered, she had been standing. Pushing the chair back, she hurried into the hallway.

"I've got it!" she called, picking up the upstairs extension.

"Hi, Lisa. Want to go Rollerblading?"

"I'd love to! Let me check with my folks."

She set down the phone and gave herself a little hug. After their discussion on the beach earlier that day, she hadn't been sure she would *ever* hear from Brian again—though once they had agreed to drop the topic of the house, things had been quite friendly.

Her happy feelings were quickly squashed. "I'm sorry, Lisa," said her mother apologetically. "But your father and I are taking your grandmother to visit some of her old island friends, and I don't want to leave Carrie alone."

Lisa's face reflected her disappointment.

"Maybe you can have Brian over here," said her mother quickly. "I don't think there would be anything wrong with that, do you, Martin?"

Lisa held her breath while her father made up his mind.

Finally he nodded and said, "I suppose it's all right, as long as Carrie is here."

Lisa scowled; she resented the implication that there would be something wrong if Carrie wasn't going to be "chaperoning" them. But she was so pleased to be able to invite Brian over that she refused to get upset by it.

"Thanks, Mom. Dad. Thanks a lot."

She sprinted back up the stairs and snatched up the phone. "It's no go," she said, panting. "But you can come over if you want to. I have to stay with Carrie and . . ." Her voice trailed off as she realized how dull it all sounded. If she had been afraid of boring him the night before, this really ought to do it.

"Is it okay with your folks?"

She was so surprised she nearly dropped the receiver. "Sure! I mean, if you really want to."

"Hey, look," Brian said. "If I didn't want to, I wouldn't." His voice suddenly turned serious. "Besides, I don't like the idea of them going off and leaving the two of you alone in that place."

Lisa was torn between gratitude and a desire to tell Brian that she could take care of herself very well, thank you, and hang up. But his self-deprecating laugh took the edge off his words. "I don't know what good it will do to have me there if anything starts up," he said. "But I'd feel better knowing you're not alone."

She smiled. "Good. We'll be waiting for you."

She set the receiver gently into the cradle. Living in a haunted house did have *some* advantages!

The video Brian had brought with him was over, the last kernel of popcorn consumed.

"Don't you think you'd better go to bed?" Lisa said to Carrie.

"What for? It's Saturday night. You're supposed to stay up on Saturday night."

Lisa threw a hopeless glance at Brian, but he was smiling. Carrie's presence didn't seem to bother him at all.

"Let's play Monopoly!" cried Carrie, as if she had just had a revelation.

"I thought you were bored sick with Monopoly," said Lisa.

"I was tired of playing with you," said her sister

airily. "It's different now that Brian's here. Too bad Gramma's not here, too. Then we could play bridge."

"I don't know how," said Brian.

"We'll teach you," replied Carrie glibly. "Then you'll be ready the next time we have a chance. I'll get the cards."

"Maybe Brian doesn't want to learn," said Lisa tartly.

"Oh, I don't mind. We'll work at it till your folks get home. Then I'll have to get going."

Lisa felt her heart sink. She was dying to spend some time alone with Brian.

"Great!" cried Carrie. "I'll be right back." She scrambled up the stairway.

"I'm sorry," said Lisa, when she was out of sight.

Brian waved his hand dismissively. "Don't be so uptight. I don't know what's worrying you. You and your sister are fun to be with. You've got a good sense of humor. You don't talk when it's not necessary. When you do say something, it makes sense. I'm having a good time. Relax, will you?"

He smiled at her. Lisa smiled back, delighted by his words.

"Here they are!" yelled Carrie, bounding down the stairs. "We couldn't have played Monopoly anyway. The board's still sticky...."

Lisa laughed and told Brian the story of the orange soda. It didn't seem possible it was only two days ago they had caused the mess.

"That was what got us started on the automatic writing," she said, finishing the tale. She paused uncomfortably. She hadn't really meant to talk about that.

Brian nodded.

54

Lisa busied herself with shuffling the cards.

Carrie looked from Lisa to Brian and back again. "You know," she said softly, "we don't have to play bridge."

Suddenly the silence grew heavier. Brian and Lisa looked at each other across the table.

"Your grandmother—" began Brian.

"Oh, come on," said Carrie. "I like Gramma, but she's not here right now." Her eyes were flashing. "What do you say?"

Lisa hesitated. It was the oddest thing. She really didn't want to stir up anything else. Yet she had a fantastic urge to follow Carrie's unspoken suggestion and try the automatic writing again. She was so curious about what someone was trying to communicate to them! Lisa glanced at Brian. He seemed distinctly uneasy. Yet she could read it in his eyes—he was curious, too. Their gazes locked. She felt a sense of challenge, and the excitement of doing something weird and dangerous together.

"Let's give it a try," he whispered.

Lisa felt a chill run down her spine. What was it that made something forbidden, something possibly dangerous, so incredibly appealing?

Without a word, she began to gather up the cards. Carrie jumped up and ran to get the paper and pencils. "It's my turn," she said when she came back. She set the paper in front of her, picked up a pencil, and said, "Will you light the candle, Brian?"

He struck a match and did as she asked. Lisa turned off the lamp nearest to the table. She left on the lamp that stood on the far side of the parlor, not wanting to take a chance on the candle going out and leaving them in total darkness.

She reached across the table and took Brian's hand. His face was intent, almost grim, and she wondered if he regretted saying yes to the experiment. She caught his eye, asking the question silently.

He shook his head. "Let's get started," he whispered.

"Take my elbows," said Carrie. "Lisa, you give the call." She closed her eyes and set the pencil on the paper, waiting expectantly.

Lisa paused for a moment, then began to speak. "O spirits from the other side, if there are any here who wish to communicate with us, now is the time. Give us your message."

They waited in silence, scarcely daring to breathe.

Nothing happened.

Carrie opened her eyes, and her disappointment was clear on her face. "I guess the spirits don't like me," she said almost bitterly.

There was a little *plink* as a drop of water fell from the ceiling.

"What was that?" cried Carrie. She looked up. Another drop struck the table. "Ohmigosh!" she yelled. "The bathtub must be running. Who turned it on? Come on, you guys!" She bolted away from the table and started up the stairs. Brian and Lisa were close behind her.

But when they reached the bathroom, they stopped. "I don't get it," said Carrie, a puzzled expression on her face. "There's no water here at all. What's going on?"

"Maybe there's a pipe leaking," said Brian.

"That could be," said Lisa. "But I don't really think so."

Brian turned to her. "Why not?"

She told him what had happened earlier that evening.

"This place is wackier than I thought," he said. Taking Lisa's hand, he headed back toward the stairway. Carrie followed close at their heels.

The ceiling was still dripping. They took their places at the table and stared at the little puddle that had formed in the center of it. Brian reached out and touched it with the tip of his finger, then placed his finger on his tongue.

He made a face. "It's not salt water," he said. "But it has a swampy taste to it. A little like a fish tank. Or at least it tastes the way a fish tank smells."

"Shhh!" said Carrie. Her eyes grew wide. She reached across the table and took Lisa's hand, squeezing it so hard that it hurt.

Lisa squeezed back. She reached out and took Brian's hand. She knew that he heard it, too.

An adult imitating a childish voice, high and piping, was calling out somewhere above them, "Mother? Mother, where are you?"

Lisa felt the small hairs on the back of her neck begin to rise. The voice stopped. Another took its place. Lisa felt a lump in her throat block the scream she wanted to release.

"Carrie?" called the voice. It was desperate. "Carrie, where are you, darling? I'm looking for you!"

Lisa looked at her sister. She was trembling, her face white with terror. Lisa could see she was struggling with herself, straining to resist some impulse.

Finally she gave in. "Here I am!" she cried at last. "Here! Here!"

The candle roared up as it had the night before.

There was a rush of wind and then another sound,

strange and unexpected. Lisa looked toward the stairway and choked back a cry of terror. Water was pouring down the steps. Green and swampy looking, it flowed like a waterfall, gathering in a pool at the base of the stairs.

"No!" roared Brian. He yanked his hand away from Lisa's and sprang to his feet. The circle was broken. Instantly the candle's flame dwindled to its normal size. The water stopped running. The puddle at the base of the stairs disappeared.

But somewhere far above her Lisa could hear the hysterical sobbing of a woman who sounded as though her heart was breaking.

She looked at Brian and Carrie.

Their faces were blank.

She didn't even need to ask. She knew that now she was the only one who could hear it.

6

A flash of light along the living room wall signaled a car entering the driveway. They could hear the sound of tires crunching on gravel.

"It's Mom and Dad!" cried Lisa. "Put these things away! I don't want them to know what we've been up to."

With a single sweep of her arm Carrie cleared the table of the incriminating pencils and paper. As she rushed to hide them, Lisa bolted for the television set and switched it on. Then all three of them scrambled for the sofa.

They settled in as the tube began to glow.

A scream pierced the night.

"Great," muttered Lisa as the front door opened. "Just what we need; a Freddy Krueger movie!"

"Lisa!" whispered Carrie. "They're never going to believe *this*!"

Lisa looked at her sister in puzzlement, then suddenly realized that she was sitting at one end of the couch, with Brian at the other, and Carrie in between! Lisa and Carrie fumbled to change places quickly and quietly. Lisa was just settling against Brian when her father walked into the room and boomed, "Hello, kids! Have a nice evening?"

Lisa flinched. She hated it when her father acted overenthusiastic in front of her friends. She knew he meant well. But it always embarrassed her.

Her mother and grandmother appeared in the doorway behind him, looking slightly frazzled.

"Hello, girls," said her mother. "Hello, Brian."

When Brian stood to greet them, Mr. Burton said in an impressed voice, "Manners! I like that."

Lisa flinched again.

Mrs. Burton stepped forward and took her husband's arm. "Come on, Martin. We're interrupting the movie."

"What? Oh, sure, sure. You kids have a good time," he said as his wife steered him toward the stairs.

Dr. Miles remained standing at the door to the living room.

"Did *you* have a good time, Gramma?" asked Carrie.

The old woman nodded. "As a matter of fact, I did. But I began to feel uneasy around the time we left. And just before we got home, I had an awful feeling that ..." She looked at them searchingly. "Are you three all right?"

Lisa and Carrie exchanged a glance. "Sure," said Lisa. "No need to worry about us!"

Dr. Miles shook her head. "I hope not." She stepped into the room and kissed each girl on the

60

cheek. "Good night, darlings. Good night, Brian. It was nice to see you again."

"Good night, Dr. Miles," Brian replied politely.

They watched as she climbed the stairs. Lisa thought, for no reason she could put her finger on, how proud she was of her grandmother.

"Whew," said Brian, when the old woman had disappeared at the top of the steps. " 'An awful feeling that something was wrong.' Is she psychic or something?"

"I'm beginning to wonder," said Lisa.

Brian sat back down. "So . . . what are you going to do?"

"About what?" replied Lisa.

Brian frowned. "Don't act stupid. Are you going to tell your parents about all this or not?"

Lisa shook her head. "Absolutely not. We're just going to stop messing around with the automatic writing."

"That won't be easy," said Carrie. "It's like potato chips—hard to stop once you get started."

"Potato chips only make you fat," said Brian. "I've got a feeling the consequences from this could be a lot worse."

Lisa grimaced. "I'll admit it was fantastically scary. But I told you yesterday I don't think there's any real danger. Nothing threatening has happened. It's only scary because we don't understand it."

"If you don't understand it, how do you know it's not dangerous?" Brian asked.

Lisa hesitated. He had her, and she knew it. "Well, it doesn't make any difference," she said at last. "I told you, we're not going to do it anymore."

61

"Let's just hope that whatever you've stirred up is also willing to stop," said Brian grimly.

As Lisa and Carrie were settling into bed later that night, Carrie said, "Do you really think there's nothing to worry about?"

Lisa looked at her sister. Her eyes were troubled, and a worried expression wrinkled her face. She wanted to lie to Carrie, to reassure her the way she had Brian. But they were in this together, and there was no sense in keeping anything from each other.

"I'm not certain," she answered, pulling back the sheets. "I don't believe Gramma's explanation that it's something psychological. Not for a minute. This place is haunted, and that's all there is to that."

Carrie shivered.

"Hey, I thought you were eager for some good stories to tell when you got home," teased Lisa.

Carrie forced a smile. "You know me—always changing my mind!"

Lisa put an arm around her. "That's right," she said soothingly. "I forgot."

Carrie leaned her head against Lisa. "Do you think she'll come back tonight?"

"I don't know," said Lisa softly. She glanced at the clock on the dresser; the lighted dial read 12:05. "It's after midnight. If she was a traditional ghost, she would have been here already."

"Maybe she's like me," said Carrie, stifling a yawn. "Always late!"

Lisa woke with a start. Where was she?

She looked around and let out a little sigh of relief. She was in her bedroom. Carrie was sleeping next to her. It was just the sudden waking out of a deep sleep that had made her feel disoriented.

But what had roused her? Something had caused her to stir from her sleep.

The piano! Someone was playing the piano.

She had a feeling she knew who it was. Sliding her feet into her slippers, she stood and put on her robe. Then she lit the candle again and headed for the hall.

I must look like the cover of a horror novel, she thought. Then, creating the advertising copy, she added, *"Stalking the darkened corridor with a candle in her hand, the fearless girl searched for the mysterious sounds."*

Lisa paused at the top of the stairs, struck by a sudden urge to turn back. *Why are you doing this, anyway?* demanded a tiny voice inside her head, speaking for the sensible part of her personality—the part she so often ignored.

It was a reasonable question. Why *was* she doing this?

Slowly an answer took shape in her mind. It was partly curiosity. She had never realized how powerful curiosity was, how it could drive you on even in the face of fear. She had heard her mother and father talking about "the human condition" one night after dinner. This must be part of it—to be controlled by curiosity, to push on when some wiser part of you was crying out, "Turn back! *Turn back!*"

That was part of it. But there was more. In the same way that the house was haunted by a ghost, Lisa was haunted by the ghost's sorrow. She had to believe that the woman who wept in the night had come back because she wanted something, *needed* something. And Lisa had the wild idea that maybe she could help solve the spirit's problem. The sound of that weeping had stayed with her since she had first heard it. It, too, was part of what drove her on now.

The piano was playing softly. Lisa hummed under her breath, trying to catch the tune. It was sweet and oddly sad. Suddenly she recognized it: "Beautiful Dreamer" by Stephen Foster. Her grandmother had often sung it to her as a lullaby when she was little. The words drifted through her head as she took her first step down the stairs.

For an instant the piano stopped, almost as if the player had sensed her presence. Then it began again, a little louder than before, yet still only a ghost of a melody, barely tickling across the threshold of her hearing.

Lisa reached the bottom of the stairs and stood for a moment in wary silence. The woman was sitting at the piano, swaying from side to side as she played. She stopped. Lisa could see her shoulders shake with sobs. Then she began to play again, and Lisa smiled in spite of herself as the merry notes of "Bill Bailey" came tinkling through the room. She almost had an urge to sing along.

Suddenly the woman slammed her hands against the keys, creating a harsh jumble of sound. She turned around on the bench and, looking up, saw Lisa. Her expression of grief shifted to one of rage, her face contorted by a fury that was almost insane. She leaped from the bench and rushed toward Lisa, her hands stretched before her.

Her anger was searing. In the same way that a light that is too bright hurts the eyes, or a noise that is too loud hurts the ears, this blast of emotion hurt some tender place inside Lisa. It was too much, too powerful, and she staggered under the weight of it.

But only briefly. For the woman was almost on her now, and Lisa's sudden terror was far greater than the pain. A scream burst from her lips, and without even realizing it she turned and scrambled up the stairs as fast as she could. Her candle swayed precariously, spattering drops of hot wax. At the top of the stairs Lisa tripped. The candle flew ahead of her, then went out. Sprawling in the darkened hallway, she screamed and screamed. She tried to get to her feet, but she was tangled in her gown and robe.

Suddenly her father was at her side. He took her by the elbow and helped her to her feet. "Lisa! Lisa, what is it?"

For a moment she was mute with horror. Gasping, shaking, she tried to tell him what had happened. Nothing would come out. She turned.

The ghost was still there!

Rage twisting those familiar features, the ghost reached past Mr. Burton and slapped Lisa across the face.

Though all she really felt was a moment of numbing cold, Lisa screamed again.

The ghost vanished.

Her father was shaking her shoulders. "Lisa! *Lisa!* What is it?"

Her mother appeared in the hall behind them. Carrie and her grandmother dashed out of their rooms as well, the concern that etched their faces making them look strangely similar.

Lisa was gasping for breath. "It was a ghost," she sobbed. "Didn't you hear it? It was playing the piano. It was angry. It was after me. Didn't you hear it?"

"Oh, for heaven's sake," said her father. "I thought you were old enough to watch those stupid films without going off the deep end. No more Freddy Krueger for you for a while, young lady!"

"Daddy! Don't you believe me?"

"I believe you had a vivid nightmare," said her father. Her mother touched his arm. His face softened, and he put an arm around Lisa, drawing her close. "I'm sorry, Lisa. My temper is on a short fuse these days. I didn't meant to be so harsh. Come on, I'll sit in your room with you for a while." He gave her a little squeeze. "But I mean it about those films!"

"But, Daddy . . ." Lisa stopped. It was no use. Nothing she could say would make her father believe what she had seen.

But she knew someone believed her. The look on her grandmother's face told Lisa that Dr. Alice Miles believed every word she had uttered.

7

*L*isa's father stayed with her until she dropped into a fitful sleep—though if Carrie had not been there, she doubted she would have slept at all. Again, she was surprised at how much it meant to have another person in the room, no matter how young and silly.

On Sunday morning while they were still sitting in bed, she told this to Carrie, who informed her—in no uncertain terms—that she was not silly at all.

"I'm sorry," replied Lisa. "Poor choice of words. I should have said 'young and ridiculous.' "

At this Carrie leaned forward, pulled her pillow from behind her back, and gave Lisa a thump.

Never one to submit to violence passively, Lisa grabbed her pillow and whacked back.

Before they knew it, the two girls were chasing each other about the room, their hysterical laughter punctuated by the dull *Thwack! Thwack!* of pillow warfare.

Lisa felt wonderful. She found herself laughing harder than she had in days as the tensions that had been building up inside were released in the wildness of the crazy pillow fight. She was on the verge of collapsing when the door swung open.

It was remarkable. Their father didn't have to say anything. He just stood there looking stern, and within seconds both girls had let their hands drop to their sides, the pillows fall to the bed.

Mr. Burton stared at each of them in turn. Following his gaze to Carrie, Lisa had to choke back a giggle. Her little sister's hair was flying in all directions. Her cheeks were red, her eyes were flashing, and she was panting like a marathon runner at the end of a race. The top of her nightgown had slid down over one shoulder.

Suddenly Lisa wondered what she looked like herself.

"I'm glad you're feeling better, Lisa," said her father, in a tone of voice that made it painfully clear she would be wise not to feel *too* much better.

He turned and left the room.

Lisa and Carrie looked at each other for a moment. Then Carrie began to giggle. Unable to control herself, she collapsed on the bed and pushed her face against her pillow. Lisa began to giggle, too. Soon both girls were lying on the bed, faces buried in their pillows, bodies shaking helplessly.

"Lisa! Carrie! Are you all right?" It was their grandmother. She took each of them by a shoulder and shook them heartily.

The girls rolled over, trying to control their laughter. Carrie's face was red. She had her lips pressed together but was giggling and sputtering anyway. That struck Lisa as indescribably funny; she rolled over and buried her face in her pillow again.

For a moment their grandmother was silent. Then she began to laugh, too.

The last few days had been hard on all three of them.

Brian called just before noon, both to see how she was and to tell her that his family was going to visit some relatives that day, so he wouldn't be able to see her. Lisa debated with herself about whether to tell him what had happened after he left the night before. Finally she decided to put it off till she could see him in person.

Or maybe put it off altogether, she admitted to herself.

She felt wistful about not being able to see him that day. On the other hand, she did need some time to herself just to think. She spent the afternoon on the beach, working on her tan and soaking up sunlight as if it were an antidote to what was happening at night in the strange old house.

Even so, she felt apprehensive when it came time to go to bed that night. She could tell Carrie felt the same way. Neither of them knew what manifestations the night might bring.

"Do you smell smoke?" Carrie asked, just as they were drifting off to sleep.

Lisa sat up. She thought she could detect a hint of smoke. But after a thorough search that managed to annoy their parents considerably, they decided it must be nothing but faint traces of a campfire on the beach, being carried to their open window by the ocean breeze.

On Monday Brian returned with his father to work on the windows. He took advantage of his lunch break to go for a walk with Lisa.

"Anything happen yesterday?" he asked anxiously as soon as they were alone.

She shook her head. "No, it was pretty quiet." She hesitated, then added, "But things sure got out of hand after you left Saturday night." Speaking quickly, she told him the story of the mysterious piano playing and the attack of the weeping woman.

Brian's face was grim, and when she finished he told her again that he thought she should get out of the old house.

"Wouldn't I love to," she answered bitterly. "I've been wanting to leave since the day we got here." She gave Brian a quick smile. "At least, until last Friday, when you showed up. But I told you what my father said. He thinks I was just having a bad dream the other night. If I press it, he'll probably figure I'm making things up because I want to go home. Like I said, he believes there's a scientific explanation for everything. And my grandmother is just as bad. Hard as a rock. Of course, she was a geologist. Talk about dealing with reality!" Lisa giggled. "The kids on campus used to call her The Great Stone Face. They also called her Rocky."

Brian looked at her for a second, then began to smile. "Rocky Miles. Not bad!"

"I figured it would appeal to your sick sense of humor," said Lisa. "Gramma was such a tough grader they called her course the Rocky Miles Endurance Test."

Brian's smile broadened. "I bet no one took it for granite."

Lisa rolled her eyes, but refused to groan. "But you want to know something weird?" she said. "I think Gramma does believe me—or at least some part of her does. You should have seen her face when I was telling Dad about the ghost." She frowned, then added in frustration, "I don't get it."

"Maybe she knows more than she's telling," suggested Brian.

"What do you mean?"

"Well, you said she used to summer here, right?"

Lisa nodded.

Brian looked away, as if he were embarrassed. Then he looked directly into her eyes. "I've been doing a little asking around. My mother told me there was an awful tragedy in your house once. She wouldn't tell me exactly what happened, though. I couldn't figure out if she didn't know, or just didn't want me to think she was gossiping. But I got the impression it's part of the village folklore that something horrible happened here a long time ago." He shrugged. "Terrible tragedy, haunted house. Every town has something like it. Only it seems as if this one is the real thing!"

"Great." Lisa moaned. "Why me?"

She grabbed a low-hanging branch and pulled down on it. It was hard to believe in ghosts on a sunny day like this. She looked down the road, a lovely country lane. The ocean air was sweet and clean, and the breeze rustled through Brian's blond hair in a way she found fantastically attractive. She let the branch support her weight as she swayed back and forth, wondering what her grandmother was hiding.

An hour later Lisa was leaning against another tree, the old oak in the front yard, and watching her grandmother. Brian was back on his ladder, working away at the windows. He had made one more pun about their "spirited discussion," then withdrawn his hand from hers and given her a quick kiss before he ran up the driveway. His father had been standing by the house, looking at his watch and frowning. Lisa hoped she hadn't gotten Brian into trouble.

Her grandmother was sitting on the porch swing, reading. Lisa smiled. The older woman was wearing jeans and a T-shirt. The shirt, a gift from one of her graduate students when she had retired, said THE GREAT STONE FACE in large black letters across the front. Dr. Miles sat cross-legged on the swing, the book perched between her knees. With her head down, it would be easy to look at her and think she was a college student studying for a summer exam. From this distance, only her white hair, done up in an old-fashioned bun, gave her away.

Brian had urged Lisa to talk to her grandmother, to see if she would open up about what had happened here so long ago.

Lisa hesitated. Gramma Miles was a dear, as sweet as could be ... when no one was crossing her. But it was not wise to press her. She had developed a sharp tongue in the classroom. She claimed it was partly a result of being one of the first women in a very male-dominated field. Whatever the reason, that sharpness often strayed over into her everyday life.

"Well, sticks and stones and all that," muttered Lisa as she tried to convince herself that finding out what was going on in the old house was too important to let herself be intimidated by the fear of a few pointed comments.

Trying to appeal casual, she started toward the porch.

Dr. Miles looked up as Lisa climbed the steps. Setting down her book, the old woman peered at her granddaughter over the rim of her glasses.

"Mind if I sit down?" asked Lisa, gesturing toward the swing.

Dr. Miles smiled. "Not at all. Glad to have you."

Lisa settled in next to her grandmother, then reached over and took the book from her lap. She grinned. Most of the women on the beach were reading whatever novel was on top of the current bestseller list. Not her grandmother. She was totally absorbed in *Oil-Bearing Properties of Devonian Shale: A Research Analysis,* by Dr. Edgar Martinson.

"Looks fascinating," said Lisa dryly.

Her grandmother chuckled. "It is, for an old rockhound like me." She patted Lisa on the knee. "Now, I know you're very fond of me. I also know that you almost never sit down just to talk."

When Lisa started to protest, her grandmother said, "Oh, baloney. It doesn't bother me that you came to sit with me for a reason. But don't try to pretend it isn't so. You've got other things on your mind, and so have I. Right now I would guess that whatever you have on your mind is something you think I can help with. So out with it. What's up?"

Lisa looked at her grandmother and thought what an odd mix she was, sometimes brusque and sometimes tender, sometimes strictly business and sometimes very silly. She liked that about her.

Steeling herself, trying not to let her voice quiver, she said abruptly, "I want to know what's going on here. Tell me what you know."

73

It was as if a curtain had been pulled across her grandmother's eyes. "What are you talking about?"

Lisa got angry. "Don't pretend you don't know, Gramma. Ever since we started that automatic writing, things have been weird in this house. And it's not coming from me!" she added defiantly, remembering what her grandmother had said about poltergeist activity.

"Lisa, you will watch your tone of voice when you speak to me," said Dr. Miles sharply.

Lisa faltered. "I . . . I'm sorry. But that doesn't change the question, Gramma. I want to know what's going on."

Dr. Miles gave Lisa an icy glare. "What's going on is this: Everyone here is under a great deal of pressure because I put us into a difficult situation. Your father has waited years to have this chance to write. Now that he does have it, he's terribly worried about whether or not he can actually do it. Your mother is dealing with the fact that she is forty-some years old and has never developed a career. She sees Carrie becoming independent and knows she won't really be needed much longer. Spending the summer in the same house with a pair of professors like your father and me only makes things that much harder on her. She doesn't like being the only adult here without a paying occupation. Of course, that was her choice. I urged her to complete school. But she was as headstrong as I am. Sometimes I think she dropped out of college just to rebel against me."

Lisa stared. This kind of truth about the family was not at all what she had been after.

"Of course, I'm slowly losing my mind because I can't stand being retired," continued Dr. Miles. "And you just plain don't want to be here. Carrie's the only one without a reason to be upset, and I imagine the rest of us are in such a state we're making life miserable for her, too. So. You want to know what's going on? There are five people in this house under a lot of strain, and they're starting to show some psychic manifestations of it. Or do you think we're actually receiving visits from the spirit world?"

The tone in which she asked the question made the possibility seem so utterly ridiculous that Lisa found herself wondering if that really was what she believed after all.

"I don't know," she said at last. Then, gathering her courage, she added, "But I do know *you* had an awfully strange expression on your face the night that ghost chased me up the stairs."

Her grandmother's eyes grew hard, and suddenly "The Great Stone Face" seemed a perfect description for her. "Lisa, I am a scientist. I don't like to talk about nonsense!"

That was it. End of conversation. Lisa knew there wasn't a chance of getting anything else out of her grandmother. She sighed and rose from the swing. "Thanks, Gramma," she said, her voice heavy with sarcasm.

Dr. Miles had opened her book. "Not at all, dear. Come and talk to me anytime."

Lisa felt as if she were going to explode.

Tuesday was much like Monday. Brian and his father finished the work on the house, and Brian asked Lisa if she would like to go out for a ride and get something to eat that night. They had a lovely evening, and avoided talking about the house at all.

Her grandmother acted as if the previous day's conversation had never taken place.

Carrie, too, seemed to have forgotten that anything had happened. Lisa knew that wasn't really so. She had learned over the last few years that Carrie would bury things inside, worry about them, chew them over, all the while acting as if they were of no concern at all—only to let them out in a sudden storm of anger or tears days later.

Her father settled down. With the rain finally over and the work on the house completed, he began to make solid progress on his book. His mood seemed to improve with every page he finished.

Mrs. Burton spent time on the beach, reading and sunning herself.

All in all, it seemed as if everything had returned to normal. Lisa should have been very happy. With Brian's arrival on the scene, the summer had taken on a new glow, and she was no longer aching to go home.

But she couldn't easily forget being chased by a ghost. Uncomfortable memories lingered in her mind. She waited with dread for the next appearance, the next manifestation of whatever was haunting the old house.

"Relax," said Carrie as they went to bed Tuesday night. "I think it's over."

Wednesday morning the puddles began to appear.

8

Lisa woke with the vague awareness that something was wrong. Drifting up from the deepest sleep she had had in several nights, she finally realized that her father was bellowing somewhere downstairs.

She rolled over. Carrie was next to her, her hair damp. Lisa frowned. She detected a strange odor in the air. She couldn't quite place it. But it wasn't right; it didn't belong in the bedroom. She sniffed curiously, but the smell seemed to be drifting away.

Downstairs her father's voice was growing louder.

Carrie sat up and stretched. "What's going on?" she asked, stifling a yawn.

"I don't know. Daddy's on the warpath about something."

"Boy, the cease-fire didn't last long, did it? Do you think we should go see what's wrong, or lie low until it blows over?"

"I don't know. It's probably safer to stay here. But my curiosity is killing me!"

"Mine, too!" said Carrie. She swung her legs over the edge of the bed and grabbed her robe. "Let's see what's up."

Martin Burton was standing in the kitchen, clutching a sheaf of soggy papers and roaring like a wounded bear. "You tell me!" he cried, shaking the papers in his wife's face. "I don't have the slightest idea!"

When the girls entered the room, he turned to them and cried, "Do you two know anything about this?"

"About what?" asked Lisa.

"This! My notes for my next chapter! I spent all yesterday afternoon working on them. Now they're soaking wet!"

Lisa and Carrie looked at each other. "We never go near your office, Daddy," said Carrie. "It's not worth the risk."

Lisa saw her grandmother try to hide a smile behind her coffee cup. The dig went by Mr. Burton unnoticed.

"Well, somebody did something in there," he growled. "When I went in this morning, I found a puddle on the desk. A puddle! And all the work I did yesterday was sitting in the middle of it, sopping wet. I would have blamed Smokey, but he was out all night. Besides, it was the wrong color."

"What do you mean?" asked Lisa.

"The water was green—almost as if it had algae in it. And it smelled like a pond."

Dr. Miles put down her coffee cup with a clatter.

Lisa felt a little twist in her stomach. Pond water. *That* was what she had smelled when she first woke this morning. She looked at Carrie. Her head was still damp. Lisa had a terrible urge to bury her face in her sister's hair and see if she could still smell that odd odor. Why did she even suspect it wasn't perspiration that had dampened Carrie's head? She restrained herself. Her parents would really think she was going off the deep end if she started sniffing her sister's hair.

"I'm awfully sorry, Daddy," said Lisa with genuine sympathy. "I don't have any idea what happened. But I'd be glad to type up some of the pages for you, if that would help. I could use the practice anyway."

Her father smiled, and it was as if a cloud had lifted from the room. "That would be great. Thanks, Lisa. I really appreciate it."

Lisa felt a warm glow inside as she went back upstairs to get dressed. She had almost forgotten how nice her father was when he wasn't so preoccupied. She was glad to be able to help him. And maybe typing would take her mind off the recent, unexplainable events.

Lisa sat at the desk in her father's office, trying to make sense of the page she was supposed to be typing. She had no idea what it said. Her father's handwriting was pretty bad to begin with. Add to that the penciled-in changes and the damage from the water, and the page was almost impossible to decipher. She was beginning to regret having volunteered for this job—especially since it was such a sunny day outside.

Plink!

She looked to her right. A drop of greenish water had appeared on the table.

Plink! Another drop struck the first, causing a small

splash. *Plink! Plink! Plink!* Three more drops fell in rapid succession, forming the beginnings of a small puddle in the middle of the desk. Lisa frowned. Pond water again. The smell was uncomfortably familiar. She recognized it at once as the odor she had detected when she first woke that morning.

"Daddy?"

No answer. She forgot; for once her father was taking a break. He had gone to the beach with the others.

She was alone in the house.

Plink!

This time the water splashed on Lisa. She flinched back as if she had been scalded. For some reason she didn't want it to touch her.

She pushed herself away from the desk. Gathering up the three pages she had already typed, she ran from the room. She slipped and nearly fell in a puddle of greenish water that lay in the hall.

"Mom? Dad?" Her voice was urgent, tinged with fear, though what she was afraid of she could not have said. She ran down the stairs.

The smell of smoke filled the living room. Dropping the papers, she began a frantic search for the source of it.

She found nothing.

Suddenly she stopped her search and stood bolt upright. The sound of crackling flames filled the room.

The smoky odor grew stronger.

Lisa looked around, her eyes wide with fear. What was going on?

She heard something in the hallway above her and held her breath, straining to catch the sound. It was the voice of the weeping woman. She was calling softly, "Carrie? Carrie, where are you? I'm coming, Carrie!"

Lisa turned and bolted from the house, slamming the door behind her. She was panting as if she had just run a mile. What was going on inside seemed impossible outside in the daylight.

She turned back. After a moment's hesitation she opened the door.

A blast of heat struck her in the face.

She screamed and slammed the door, then raced down the driveway as if the Hounds of Hell were at her heels.

As she ran she looked back over her shoulder to see if she was being followed—then suddenly hit something solid. A moment later she was lying on the gravel of the driveway, aching in half a dozen places.

Brian was lying next to her.

"What's wrong with you?" he asked angrily, standing and dusting himself off. He was wearing cutoff jeans, and had scraped one knee badly when he fell.

Then he saw the expression on her face. "Hey," he said, kneeling and taking her by the shoulders. "What's going on?"

She looked at him and suddenly realized who it was. "Brian!" she cried, throwing her arms around his neck. For the first time since the manifestations had begun, she started to cry.

Brian hugged her against his shoulder for a moment, letting her sob out her fear. When her tears had subsided, he pushed her away and took her chin in his hand. "All right," he said, looking her in the eyes. "Out with it. What's going on?"

Her voice shaking, Lisa gasped out the story of what had just taken place in the house.

Brian frowned. "That is genuinely weird," he said at last. "Especially the part about the voice calling for Carrie." His face grew hard. "Now do you believe me that you've got to get out of there?"

"Sure!" said Lisa angrily. "Now do you want to tell me how? Or do *you* want to be the one to explain to my father that we're living in a haunted house?"

"I'd be glad to," said Brian fiercely. He paused, and his shoulders slumped. "I see what you mean." Just as quickly his face brightened. "Stay here. I'll be back in a few minutes." He started back toward the house.

"Where are you going?" cried Lisa, running to catch up with him.

"Inside. If that stuff is still going on, I want to see it myself. Then I'll be glad to talk to your father. If it happens to both of us, maybe he will believe it!"

Lisa put a hand on his arm. "Brian, don't. It might be even worse now."

He shook her hand away. "And it might be even worse than that tonight or the next night. Who knows what could happen if you stay here?" He smiled. "But it doesn't seem quite so spooky in the daylight, so I'd just as soon check things out now." He turned up the long driveway and strode purposefully toward the house.

Lisa hesitated for a moment, then ran to catch up with him. "If you're going in, so am I," she said, taking his hand.

He started to object, looked at her face, and decided to say nothing. Together they stepped onto the porch, Lisa gripping his hand tightly.

They stood for a moment, staring at the door, won-

82

dering what they would find on the other side. Lisa shuddered; she felt as if she were standing at the gateway to the underworld.

Brian put his free hand on the doorknob. "Ready?" he asked, giving her fingers a squeeze.

She nodded.

He turned the knob and opened the door.

9

They found nothing at all out of the ordinary. No strange smells. No unexpected sounds. No disembodied spirits.

Lisa didn't know whether to be disappointed, or relieved.

Clutching Brian's hand, she followed him through the living room.

He looked around. "If I hadn't been here for all the fireworks on Saturday night, I wouldn't believe you now," he said softly.

It seemed strange to whisper in the middle of an open room in broad daylight. But Lisa understood. Despite the fact that everything seemed so normal now, something about speaking out loud seemed uncomfortable, inappropriate.

"Let's go upstairs," she whispered.

Brian nodded and led the way.

"My father's office is at the end of the hall," she said when they reached the top step. She frowned. From where they were standing, she could see that the puddle she had slipped in was gone. "It's hopeless," she said with a sigh. "We'll never get any evidence out of this."

"I'm afraid you're right," said Brian grimly. Nevertheless, he began walking cautiously down the hallway.

"I don't remember closing the door to the office," said Lisa as they approached it.

Brian stopped. "Do you want to go in?" he asked. His voice had a nervous edge that Lisa found disconcerting. She hesitated for a moment, then nodded.

"Okay," he said. "Here we go." Taking a deep breath, he swung the door open—then leaped back with a startled cry as something hurtled out of the room.

Lisa screamed, then began to laugh.

It was Smokey.

The gray cat stared at them, fur bristling, back arched.

Lisa reached for Brian's hand again. "Something has him really spooked," she said.

Brian had sagged against the wall outside the office. "Something has *him* spooked? What about me? I think I just lost ten years off my life!"

They both looked at the half-open door. After a moment Brian stepped forward and entered the room.

Nothing.

Nothing except the steady *plink, plink, plink* of green water dripping from the ceiling.

* * *

Forty-five minutes later Mr. Burton was staring angrily at the puddle on his desk. "I just don't get it," he said. He looked at the ceiling again. "Where the heck is it coming from?"

"Maybe there's a pipe running over the room?" suggested Mrs. Burton.

"If there is, the plumber must have been potted," snapped Mr. Burton.

Mrs. Burton lapsed into silence. Lisa glanced at her grandmother and caught her breath. Dr. Miles had been staring at her, but when Lisa turned in her direction, she had quickly shifted her gaze. Not quickly enough to hide her feelings, though; Lisa had caught the expression in her eyes.

The only word to describe it was fear.

"I can't make head nor tail of it," said Mr. Burton, scratching his bald spot.

At that moment the dripping stopped. The group exchanged puzzled glances.

"Well, that takes care of that," said Mr. Burton heartily. "Brian, help me move this desk, would you? I'd just as soon not have to worry about it if the dripping starts again. And ask your dad if he'll come over to take a look at the roof tomorrow. Maybe there's a spot up there that's trapping water somehow."

As they started to move the desk, the phone rang. Lisa's mother went to answer it.

"Now," said Mr. Burton, when he and Brian had repositioned the desk. "I want to talk to the two of you."

Lisa's heart sank. She knew there was no chance he was going to buy any of what she had to say.

"Alice?" said Mr. Burton meaningfully, glancing at his mother-in-law.

86

Dr. Miles nodded. "Come on," she said to Carrie. Carrie scowled fiercely but followed her grandmother out of the room.

Once the door had closed Mr. Burton sat down behind his desk. He looked out the window for a moment, then turned back to Lisa and Brian. Folding his hands in front of him, he said, "Let me start by thanking you for your relatively calm behavior on the beach. Considering what you were trying to tell me, you were remarkably restrained."

Lisa smiled at Brian. She had been proud of the way he had approached her father when they went to get the family. He had managed to be respectful but urgent, convincing Mr. Burton that it was indeed important for him to come back to the house. She wasn't sure what Brian had said to him on the walk back; the two of them had moved ahead of the rest of the group and had talked softly.

"However ... that doesn't mean I believe for a minute what you're trying to tell me," said Mr. Burton.

He looked at his daughter. "You, I'm surprised at. I'm a scientist. Your grandmother is a scientist. And somehow you've come out a mystic!" He made a noise in his throat, a sound reserved for things that truly disgusted him. "You know as well as I do that this spirit stuff is nonsense. There's a perfectly reasonable explanation for anything that happens in this world. It may not be evident at first, but it's there. No matter how strange an event seems, if you investigate it carefully enough, you can find the cause behind it. This dripping ceiling for instance. Offhand, I can think of half a dozen reasons that would provide a rational explanation—"

He was interrupted by the door swinging open.

Lisa's mother poked her head into the room. Her eyes were red, her cheeks wet with tears. "Martin, I have bad news. Jack Wilson is on the phone. Dr. Graham died last night. He had a heart attack. The family would like you to deliver the eulogy."

"Peter Graham?" asked Lisa, even as she felt tears well up in her own eyes. Dr. Peter Graham had been a close friend of the Burton family for more than a dozen years, popping in almost every day to swap stories, gossip about the college, or just mooch a meal. Lisa was shocked. How could he just die like that?

Mr. Burton looked as stunned as Lisa felt. He pushed himself away from his desk and left the room without another word.

Brian said a quiet farewell to Lisa, then slipped away from the house to let the Burtons deal with their grief in private.

An hour later the family held a meeting. After some discussion it was decided that Mr. and Mrs. Burton would take the late-afternoon ferry to the mainland, and then fly back to the college for the funeral. Carrie and Lisa would stay on the island with Dr. Miles.

Both girls had wanted very much to go home, too. But time problems made driving impossible, and plane fare for the entire family was simply more than they could afford.

Lisa and Carrie had accepted that, though it made them unhappy. Lisa had been tempted to plead with her parents to take her with them. But she had restrained herself, knowing they had enough on their minds as it was. Besides, she also knew there was no way she was going to convince them she needed to go to a funeral at home just to get away from a ghost here.

She was stuck.

The day brightened somewhat when Brian reappeared in the late afternoon with a bag of groceries and a bottle of wine.

"This is for you," he said, handing the wine to Dr. Miles. "From my parents."

He carried the groceries into the kitchen. "Mom thought it would be nice if I cooked dinner for all of you. She said you've got enough on your minds as it is."

Then he shooed them all out of the kitchen.

Lisa had been skeptical until she put the first forkful of chicken into her mouth. Then her eyes widened in surprise. It was very tasty! She found herself slightly jealous as she realized Brian was a much better cook than she was.

She looked over at him. He winked and smiled back.

"Hey, this is good!" exclaimed Carrie, her surprise all too obvious.

Brian laughed. "You don't have to sound like it's such a shock!"

For a moment the tension was broken. But before long, gloom had settled over the table again.

After dinner they played bridge, Carrie and Lisa patiently teaching Brian how to count and bid. As it turned out, he had a mathematical mind that took to the game. He and Dr. Miles played as partners and beat the two girls rather badly.

At eleven o'clock he left for home. Lisa could tell he was reluctant to go. But her grandmother had made it clear it was time for him to head out, so he went. He and Lisa spent a little time on the front porch before he left, holding hands and looking at the stars until Dr. Miles flicked the porch lights on and off, signaling that it was time for Lisa to get back inside.

"I don't feel good about leaving you," he said.

Lisa smiled. "That's nice. But there's not much we can do about it. I doubt your mother would let you spend the night!"

Brian laughed ruefully. "Probably not. I don't think your grandmother would go for it, either." He took both her hands. "Will you call me if anything happens? If you need me? I'll come as fast as I can. I'll even get my dad to come with me."

Lisa squeezed his hands. "Thanks. I'll keep that in mind. But we'll be all right." Hearing the lost note in her own voice, the fear that she couldn't quite hide, she shrugged and added, "I hope."

Lisa sat up in her bed and shivered. What a bizarre dream! She felt so odd.

She shook her head. The strange feeling persisted. It wasn't a dream at all! Something—or someone— was trying to communicate with her. She wasn't sure *how* she knew that, but she had no question that it was what she was feeling.

She looked at Carrie, who was sleeping with one arm flopped across her forehead. Her fingers were twitching restlessly, and her lips moved as if she were talking to herself.

Lisa wondered what was happening in her sister's dreams.

She flinched. She had just felt it again. Something

90

was definitely after her, compelling her to go to the desk, pick up the pencil—and let a message come in.

She clutched the covers. She didn't want to do it. She wanted to bury her head under the sheet and pretend nothing was happening.

But she couldn't. The call, the urging, was too insistent.

She had to go to the desk.

She flung aside the sheet. Smokey hissed as she got out of bed and just missed stepping on his head. Not bothering with robe or slippers, she hurried to the desk and sat down.

The paper and pencil lay there, almost as if they had been set out for her use.

She froze. Downstairs someone was playing the piano. The melancholy strains of "Beautiful Dreamer" drifted up to her ears.

She tried to get up from the desk, but her body wouldn't respond.

Carrie tossed restlessly and began to whimper in her sleep.

Still fighting to avoid picking up the pencil, Lisa let out a gasp of surprise. The piano music had changed. She was not musically trained, but her ear was keen enough to know that she was now hearing a duet!

Her hand trembled as it reached for the pencil. Two ghosts downstairs, one up here compelling her to write. Could there really be three ghosts in the house?

Suddenly there was no more time to think about it. Her hand grabbed the pencil and began to write.

The music tinkled. Carrie thrashed on the bed. And Lisa's hand moved firmly, decisively, across the page.

When it stopped, Lisa collapsed over the writing,

like a rag doll dropped onto the floor. Her forehead was soaked with perspiration.

After a moment she pushed herself away from the desk. She picked up the paper. The moonlight streaming through the window gave her sufficient light to read by.

A shiver made its way along her spine. The message was written in large, bold letters, the handwriting noticeably different from the first communication they had received.

But even more frightening than the form of the message was its content:

DANGER. GET CARRIE OUT.
YOU MUST LEAVE THIS PLACE AT ONCE!!!

Trembling, Lisa put the paper down.

Now what was she supposed to do?

Carrie still tossed and turned, moaning in her sleep.

Lisa decided to wake her grandmother. Scientist or not, skeptic or not, she was the adult here, and she was going to have to do something. They couldn't stay in this house any longer.

She took the paper and stepped into the hall. The piano was still playing. Lisa rubbed her arms, trying to smooth down the gooseflesh.

The ghosts were playing "Bill Bailey" again. Lisa smiled. It was such a lively song. Almost against her will, she found herself heading for the stairway. Then she remembered the last incident and was afraid. Yet the music sounded so happy that it seemed nothing frightening could be lurking below.

She made her way down the steps, stopping on the last one.

Two figures were seated at the piano. One was a woman, the same one who had attacked her a few nights ago. The other was a man, dressed in an elegant silk robe. They sat side by side, pounding on the piano, filling the room with the raucous notes of "Bill Bailey." Lisa found herself smiling.

Then she felt a hand on her shoulder.

The music died at the sound of her scream. The spirits turned in shock, then vanished.

Lisa's grandmother put her other hand on Lisa's hair and stroked it. "I'm sorry I frightened you, child." She swallowed. "I just needed to touch something real."

"You heard it?" asked Lisa.

Her grandmother nodded.

"You saw them?"

She nodded again, a distant look in her eye.

Lisa felt as if they had switched places. She saw something childish in her grandmother now, something small and scared that needed protection.

But Carrie needed protection, too.

"Then let's not play games anymore," said Lisa firmly. "You know what's going on here. You know who haunts this place. Tell me!"

Dr. Miles nodded, and Lisa could see a world of sorrow in her eyes. Tears rolling down her cheeks, the old woman whispered, "It's my mother."

10

"**S**o foolish," said Dr. Miles, reaching out and brushing her fingers against Lisa's cheek. "Young and foolish. Old and foolish. Each of us so foolish."

Lisa took her grandmother's hand in hers. The skin was rough and dry, but the hand was filled with life. "What do you mean?" she whispered.

"Both of us," said Dr. Miles. "But mostly me. Foolish pride, foolish rationality. I don't know what I was trying to prove, coming back here, bringing you all back with me. Is this house haunted? I guess it must be. I know it has haunted me for over half a century— nestled in my mind like a worm in an apple, hidden away and gnawing at the core of things."

Lisa shivered at the gruesome analogy. After a moment of silence she squeezed her grandmother's hand.

"Why?" she whispered. "Why does it haunt you?"

Dr. Miles sighed. "Four of the people I loved most in all the world died here."

Lisa shivered again. It seemed to her that was reason enough for any house to be haunted. Putting her hand on her grandmother's back, she whispered, "Let's go upstairs."

Dr. Miles walked beside Lisa docilely, like a child who had just been scolded. They went into the old woman's room.

"Get into bed," said Lisa.

Her grandmother nodded and sat on the edge of her mattress. Lisa was beginning to wonder if she would have to lift the old woman's legs onto the bed for her when Dr. Miles seemed to come back to herself. She put a pillow behind her back, tucked her legs under the covers, then patted the spot next to her.

Lisa went to the far side of the bed and climbed up next to her grandmother. Sitting cross-legged, she tucked her feet underneath her and pulled the edge of the coverlet across her knees.

"Tell me about it," she ordered.

Her grandmother looked small. Sitting up against the head of the bed, her unbound hair spread across her shoulders, she stared into the distance, her eyes blank and unfocused. Lisa had the feeling that even though she was looking across the room, she was not seeing the mirror on the wall or the fastidiously tidy dresser. She was looking into the past and remembering whatever it was she had tried so desperately to forget.

Smokey wandered into the room and jumped up between them. Dr. Miles reached out and began to stroke the gray cat. For a moment there was no sound but Smokey's rumbling purr.

Finally Dr. Miles began to speak. Her voice was small and tired sounding, and Lisa had to strain to hear her.

"It happened in 1935, when I was twelve years old. We had summered here from the time I was about two. My mother, my father, myself—and my little sister, Carrie. Times were different then. We had managed to escape the Depression, and in fact were better off than you and your parents. We had servants to take care of things—a maid and a cook who came during the day. And a nurse who lived in, taking care of Carrie and me.

"My mother was a sick woman. I didn't recognize it at the time. Oh, I did, I suppose. But it's not something you admit to yourself easily. Even less so, in those days. She was physically sick, frail and quickly exhausted. But her sickness was deeper than that, really. She was afraid of almost everything. Afraid of dying. Afraid of living. God knows what went on in her own childhood to make her that way. But that's the way she was.

"I loved her anyway, without reservation, as children do.

"Despite my mother's illness, my early childhood was happy. That was before the Depression arrived. A kind of giddiness seemed to infect the whole country then. We were mindlessly happy, it seems to me now. But it was wonderful at the time. And when you're that age, what do you know about those things anyway? Happy is happy."

She gave Lisa a wan smile and squeezed her hand. "The time you've had for growing up in hasn't been quite so sweet," she said sadly. "Oh, I don't think it's

96

been all that bad for you. But the shadows are longer now than they were then. It all changed in 1945."

Lisa gave her a puzzled look.

"Oh, study your history, child. That was the year we blew up Hiroshima and Nagasaki, and learned that our planet was as mortal as we are. I always thought a great dividing line was drawn then. No one born after that time can understand what it was like to grow up without that shadow.

"But that's beside the point. We were here. And except for an occasional episode involving my mother, we were happy. . . ."

As Dr. Miles continued the story, Lisa felt herself drawn into the past, absorbed by the web of sorrow and despair that had wrapped itself around her grandmother's happy childhood all those years ago.

Myra Halston was beautiful. Pale and too slender, she nevertheless projected an air of elegance and vulnerability that attracted men, whether she wanted to or not.

Her husband, Harrison, was a successful stockbroker, and she was the one great treasure of his life. In no sense was she a helpmate; she was far too frail for that. To Harrison Halston she was like a rare orchid, delicate and lovely and needing special care. So every summer he brought her to Sayers Island because the doctors had told him that sea air would do her good. He built her a house and hired servants to make sure she was not overworked. He did his best to ease her troubled mind.

But his best was not good enough, especially when outside events came crashing in on them.

Ellen McCormack was Carrie and Alice's nurse, and

the two girls loved her desperately. She was everything their mother was not: Large and robust, she seemed to burst with good humor and was always ready for an expedition or to tell a story.

Alice and Carrie loved their mother in the way that children love something distant and precious. But she was too fragile for them to touch, and so they gave most of their affection, their boisterous hugs, to Ellen.

Myra Halston saw this, and it hurt. She began to hate Ellen McCormack. That hatred festered like a growing infection until it poisoned her thoughts.

The simple solution would have been to let the woman go. There were plenty of others who would have welcomed the job. But Myra Halston knew her children would mourn the loss of their beloved nurse, and she did not want that to happen. She was torn between her desire to regain what she thought she had lost and her eagerness to keep her children happy.

She began to do small things to make Ellen McCormack's life miserable. She concocted stories to turn her husband against the woman. She would call Ellen into social gatherings, then humiliate her in front of the guests with carefully worded questions. At the same time she tried to buy back her children's affection with increasingly lavish gifts, not realizing she had never really lost their love to begin with.

But it was when she tried to do what she could not, tried to take Ellen McCormack's place, that the trouble really began. She was simply not able to handle the stress. She would play with the girls and end up panting and exhausted, lying on the sofa and fanning herself pathetically.

The children came to dread these episodes. It terrified them to see their mother so ill.

And then Carrie died.

Myra Halston blamed Ellen McCormack for her daughter's death because the child had drowned while the nurse was not watching her. Myra's sorrow was made more bitter by the fact that Carrie had drowned in a small fish pond that Myra herself had begged her husband to install only a year before. Playing in the backyard, Carrie had tripped, knocked her head against a rock at the edge of the pool, and fallen in, unconscious.

They found her at the pool's edge, her golden hair floating on the water, the curious fish nudging against her open, staring eyes.

That was when Myra Halston went mad indeed. She threw herself at the nurse and tried to scratch her eyes out. Her husband had had to pull her off and hold her arms while the nurse fled to the house with the weeping Alice.

For weeks after that, the cries of Myra Halston echoed through the night as she wept and wept for the lost Carrie. She shoved Alice out of her life; it was too painful for her to see the remaining child, reminding her so much of the one she had lost.

She blamed the nurse; she blamed her husband for not being there when the tragedy had occurred; she blamed Alice for being in the kitchen instead of the backyard with her sister; and she blamed the cook and the maid and the gardener, all of whom she thought should have been there when Carrie met her doom.

The doctor came twice a day to give her an injection to calm her. Alice watched with terrified eyes as he passed grimly in and out of her mother's room, shaking his head.

Each time he left, things would be quiet for a while.

But all too soon Myra's shrieks and curses would ring out once more.

Everyone in the house walked quietly, every eye held a haunted look. They had all loved Carrie, who had been a golden child, as joyful and vibrant as her mother was sickly. Her loss affected each of them deeply—and continued to affect them because of Myra Halston's madness.

Then one day Myra stepped from her room, and though her eyes were larger and darker than ever, she was calm and beautiful. For a few moments it seemed that all was well.

She crossed to her remaining daughter and took her in her arms. "I'm sorry, my darling," she said. "I've been away too long. Did you miss me?"

Alice looked at her with wide eyes. "Yes, Mother," she said. "I missed you terribly."

"That's good to hear," crooned Mrs. Halston. "I missed you, too, Carrie."

Alice began to scream. She beat at her mother's face. "I'm not Carrie! I'm not! I'm Alice! Carrie is dead!"

Her mother slapped her. Alice staggered back against the wall. Her mother's eyes went wide with recognition and with horror. "You're *not* Carrie!" she cried. "Get away from me. Get away! Get away!"

Myra Halston stood for a moment, her breast heaving, her eyes wild. Then she crumpled to the floor.

She was carried back to her room, where her grieving husband sat by her bed for the days and nights that followed.

* * *

"Oh, Gramma," whispered Lisa. "I'm so sorry."

Her grandmother squeezed her hand. "That was a long time ago," she said huskily.

"What happened next?" Lisa asked, after a moment of silence.

She could feel her grandmother stiffen beside her. "My mother sank completely into her madness. She began to hallucinate. She would imagine herself drowning as Carrie had drowned. I could hear her in her bedroom, gasping and choking and crying out for help. Then she would faint, and all would be silent for a while—until the next spell.

"Sometimes she claimed Carrie was still alive but lost. Other times she claimed Carrie was dead, and her ghost was in the bedroom with her, haunting her, and would not let her rest. Sometimes she cried out that the walls were closing in on her, green and dripping with algae.

"I was not allowed to see her very often. She wasn't eating well, and she couldn't sleep. She continued to lose weight. Her eyes grew darker and more sunken by the day.

"And yet somehow she remained beautiful. It was as if her tormented spirit was a candle burning within her failing frame, and the more it consumed, the more it illuminated her. There was something ethereal about her during that time, something unbelievably lovely." Dr. Miles paused, groping for words. "She was like a vessel that had been filled with moonlight," she said at last.

Lisa nodded. In some strange way she understood.

"It always frightened me when I had to go in and see her," continued Dr. Miles. "After that first episode I never knew how she was going to react to me. She never called me Carrie again. But sometimes she was delighted to see me and would throw her arms around me, and other times she would simply cry out and ask to have me taken from the room because I reminded her of Carrie.

"Father kept Ellen McCormack on to care for me because he could not do it himself. All his attention was given to Mother. He never blamed Ellen for what happened, and he needed her help. But we had to keep Ellen's presence a secret from my mother. Sometimes when she was having a spell, she would curse Ellen for letting Carrie die. I can remember seeing Ellen then, her face white, the tears falling. It's doubtful Carrie loved Ellen as much as she loved our mother, no matter what Mother thought. But I'm certain Ellen loved Carrie every bit as much as my mother had.

"Mother took to wandering the house at night, searching for Carrie. She claimed she could hear her, that Carrie was calling her to come and rescue her."

Again Dr. Miles tightened her grip on Lisa's hand. Lisa looked at her grandmother, whose eyes were focused on the past once more, wide and bright with remembered horror.

"She would mimic Carrie's voice. I would hear her roaming around, crying out in childish tones, 'Mother? Mother, where are you? Come and rescue me, Mother.'

"Then she would switch to her own voice and call back, 'I'm coming, Carrie. I'm coming for you.'"

Dr. Miles shuddered. "I would lie in bed, shaking with terror that she would come into my room and think I was Carrie. But she never did. Once she opened my door and peered in. But when she saw me lying there, she began to scream. She slammed the door, and I could hear my father come running up the stairs. They scuffled, and then I heard a little cry that let me know she had fainted.

"I think Ellen McCormack and my father grew closer than they should have in that time. He was so weary with caring for my mother, and they were both so burdened by the loss of Carrie that there was a natural sympathy between them. But Mother never knew about this; she didn't even know Ellen still worked for us.

"It was Mother's midnight wanderings that caused the final tragedy." Dr. Miles paused. "Fire and water. Those were the things that took my family. Carrie by water; the rest by fire."

Her hand lay limp in Lisa's, as if the telling had exhausted her.

"That last night Mother was wandering the house, calling out first in Carrie's voice, then in her own. I was in bed, quaking in fear, as usual; afraid that my door would open and I would see her again, the person I most loved and feared in all the world.

"She was carrying a candle, I was told later, and she was too lost in madness to be careful. She stopped to stare out a window, I believe. Perhaps she thought Carrie was out in the yard waiting for her. Anyway, the candleholder was later found on a windowsill.

"The curtains caught first." Dr. Miles's voice sank to a whisper. "The curtains caught, then her night-dress. She began to scream, which was not unusual. But there was something different in her voice this time, something that terrified me in a way I had not felt before. I jumped from my bed and threw open my door. I saw my mother standing in the hall, her clothes blazing around her, her skin blistering. Her long hair looked like some hellish halo, a crown of flame around her face."

Dr. Miles stopped for a minute, and Lisa was not sure she would be able to go on. She was panting, her breast heaving as if she were not merely telling the story, but reliving it.

"The last thing I remember of my mother was her looking me in the eye, her own eyes glazed with madness, and crying out, 'You let your sister die!'

"Then Father came hurtling up the stairs and knocked her down. She screamed and screamed as he tried to beat out the flames. By this time the hallway itself was on fire. I was screaming, too.

"Ellen McCormack had come out of her room and was trying to help Father.

" 'Get Alice!' he cried to her. 'Take care of Alice!'

"But the smoke had gotten to Ellen. She toppled down herself.

"I went and hid in my closet, as children sometimes do during a fire. I was lucky. When I woke up two days later, I found that the fire department had come in time to save the house and me. But that was all. My father, my mother, and Ellen were all dead.

"I was utterly alone.

"There was some money, fortunately. Father had established a trust fund for me in his will. A friend of the family was appointed my guardian. This house was sold, as was our home in the city. I was sent to a boarding school, and ... well, you pretty much know the rest. But that's the story of this house, Lisa. And if there is any place that has a right to be haunted, I think this is it." She swallowed heavily. "I don't know why I brought us all back here. Maybe I thought somehow I could finally get it out of my head. You don't know how it has haunted me, Lisa; how it waits in the back of my mind, past all my science, all my walls. You can't imagine how it hur ... hur—"

Suddenly the old woman began to shake. Her tears burst forth, streaming down her cheeks.

Lisa gathered her grandmother into her arms and let her cry on her shoulder, weeping for lost childhood and lost innocence, and for a mother she had never really known.

Somewhere in the distance she could hear another voice weeping, too.

Then Carrie began to scream.

11

Dr. Miles bolted out of her bed. Lisa came scrambling after her, tripping on her nightgown and lurching to her feet again. They shot down the hall and burst through the door of the room that Lisa and Carrie shared.

Carrie sat upright in bed, her face distorted with terror. Her hair was soaking wet.

"Mommy!" she was screaming. "Mommy, help me!"

Lisa threw her arms around her sister. "Carrie!" she crooned. "Carrie, it's all right. It's me, Lisa."

Carrie continued to scream, until Dr. Miles reached forward and gave her a solid slap across the face. Carrie gasped, but suddenly her eyes seemed to focus. "Gramma!" she cried, throwing herself forward and flinging her arms around her grandmother's neck. She began sobbing on the old woman's shoulder, much as Dr. Miles herself had been sobbing on Lisa's shoulder just moments before.

"It's all right, sweetheart," whispered Dr. Miles. "We're with you. Lisa and I are here."

Slowly Carrie's sobs began to subside. She pulled away from her grandmother and looked at Lisa. "You *weren't* here," she said accusingly.

"I was with Gramma," said Lisa, swamped by guilt. "We were talking."

Carrie rubbed her nose on her arm. "I'm sorry," she snuffled. "I just had such an awful nightmare."

The moonlight spilling through the window made puddles on the floor and across the bed. Carrie sat in a pool of it, drenched by the light—and by something else.

The rank smell of pond water filled Lisa's nostrils as Carrie took her hand. "I was drowning," she whispered. "I was drowning and I couldn't breathe." She shuddered. "The fish were poking at my eyes. I screamed for Mommy, but she didn't come. I screamed and screamed, but he wouldn't let me up." She started to cry again.

Looking over Carrie's shoulder, Lisa caught her grandmother's eye. "What do you mean, *he* wouldn't let you up?"

Carrie shook her head. "I don't know! I was drowning. He wouldn't let me up." Her sobbing was softer now. The tears rolled slowly down her cheeks. "It was awful. Lisa, I'm scared."

Lisa enfolded her sister in her arms. Carrie lay against her, shivering occasionally, sniffing, and crying. After a time she was silent. Her body relaxed, and she began to sleep soundly again.

Dr. Miles pulled a chair beside the bed and sat holding her younger granddaughter's hand.

When the dawn light came spilling over the windowsill, she was still there.

At nine o'clock that morning Alice Miles marched
Lisa and Carrie out of the house and into the village
to the library, where they proceeded to take out as
many books on spirits, ghosts, and haunted houses as
the bemused librarian would allow.

"The only way to fight something is to understand
it," pronounced Dr. Miles as she led the girls back to
the house. "I spent too much time denying what was
happening because it didn't fit my version of reality.
My mistake, and a big one. Now I've accepted it, with
humble apologies to you, Lisa. So. It's time we did
something."

"Why don't we just get out?" asked Lisa.

Dr. Miles looked as if the idea had never occurred
to her. She faltered for a moment. "Is that what you
want?" she asked at last.

Lisa looked at Carrie. Carrie looked at her grandmother. "Are we in danger?" she asked softly.

"I don't know. That's why we went to the library
this morning." She patted the pile of books she carried. "I'm still a novice when it comes to ghosts and
hauntings. Let's find out."

The phone was ringing when they entered the
house.

Lisa rushed to pick it up.

"Whew!" said Brian. "I was just getting ready to
head over and see if you were all right." He paused.
"Are you?"

Lisa glanced at her grandmother. "I guess so," she said softly.

"Anything happen last night?"

"It was a little rough. They were up and at it again."

"They?"

"Yeah. There are three that I'm sure of. Possibly four in all."

"Lisa, are you serious?"

"Dead serious." She grimaced. "Sorry. Bad choice of words. I got the whole story from Gramma last night. It's pretty wild. She told Carrie this morning. It really shook her up."

"Can I come over?"

Lisa checked with her grandmother. "Sure. Gramma says you can help us do some ghost research. The more the merrier."

Dr. Miles, Carrie, and Lisa were sitting at the kitchen table, surrounded by books, when Brian arrived. He took a seat across from Dr. Miles. He didn't pick up a book, however. Instead he looked at Dr. Miles and said flatly, "You've got to get out of here."

"Young man, I don't 'got' to do anything!"

Lisa had to give Brian credit. He was standing up to her grandmother's steely glare better than most students had ever been able to. "Then stay," said Brian. "That's your choice. But send Lisa and Carrie someplace else, for their sakes."

Lisa caught her breath. She could see he had scored with that shot.

Dr. Miles hesitated. "I have led a rich life," she said at last. "It has been remarkably interesting and full of surprises. The primary reason is the fact that I have never run away from anything I didn't understand. I don't think it does any good—and I don't want to train my granddaughters to be that way." She paused. "Now, do you want to help? Or would you rather head out?"

Brian and Dr. Miles locked eyes. Their gazes held for what seemed an eternity. Finally Brian broke the contact.

He looked hopelessly at Lisa.

Then he reached forward and took a book.

At noon Lisa left the table and began to put together some lunch—chicken sandwiches made with leftovers from the previous night's meal. The other three stayed at their seats, absorbed in their reading. Occasionally one of them would mark a page with a paper clip from the box Dr. Miles had set in the center of the table, or make a note with the pencils that Carrie had gathered for all of them.

Lisa smiled. The pile of books beside her grandmother had shifted from her left side to her right. She was moving through them at a remarkable pace. Lisa wished she could read like that. She looked fondly at Brian and Carrie. It was almost laughable. How many people would head for the library when faced with a problem like this?

"Well," said Dr. Miles, slamming shut the fifth book she had completed that morning, "I don't think we have anything to worry about!"

Brian looked up. "Weird as it is, I think you may be right. As near as I can make out, what you've got here are a bunch of restless spirits; scary as hell if you're not used to this kind of thing—"

"And who is?" interjected Carrie.

"But not really dangerous," continued Brian, as if he had not been interrupted.

"That's what I think, too," said Dr. Miles. "It's classic stuff: tragic deaths and unresolved conflicts. So they stay here in the house where they died, rather than moving on to the next world where they belong. They haven't been able to let go—"

"Well, whatever it's about, it's weird to be haunted by your own great-grandmother," interrupted Carrie. She made an exaggerated shiver.

"How would you like to be me?" snapped Dr. Miles. "Imagine being haunted by your own mother!"

"What about the night she chased me?" asked Lisa, coming over to the table with a platter of sandwiches. "That didn't seem so harmless."

"Did she hurt you?" asked Dr. Miles.

"No. But she tried to slap me!"

"And you didn't feel it. See, they can't really touch you. As for the slap, I think it was actually intended for me. There are some interesting parallels here. As a matter of fact, I think what really stirred them up was having Carrie in the house."

"Me?"

"Well, certainly. It was the death of the original Carrie that started everything. The spirits haven't been all that active. Otherwise this house would have a bigger reputation than it does. But it makes sense that when another young girl named Carrie moved in—a girl who, you might as well know, closely resembles the first Carrie—it would upset them. Add to that the fact that the two of you are about as far apart in age as Carrie and I were, and it's easy to see why my mother would be confusing our Carrie with the first Carrie, and you with me, Lisa. I suspect she has never gotten over her anger with me for living when Carrie died. So it wasn't you she was after at all. But she doesn't recognize me as her daughter, because I'm too old. She's trapped in the past, has no sense of how much time has gone by since that tragedy."

"That makes sense, I suppose," said Lisa. "But what about the messages?"

"Well, the first one must have been from your great-grandmother," said Brian. " 'Welcome home'—it makes a lot of sense if she thought Carrie had come back. But what about the night I was here? That one said 'Danger!' "

"I've been thinking about that," said Dr. Miles. "Believe me, it's been preying on my mind. I can think of a couple of possibilities. The one that seems to make the most sense is that it's from Ellen McCormack. She, too, is looking at Carrie as the original. She's trying to warn her away. Past, present, and future are jumbled together in their minds. She sees Carrie alive now, but she's afraid for what has already happened to her. That's the reason for the message Lisa got last night."

"I think I've got it!" said Brian. "I've been trying to figure out the first séance we did together. It seemed like such a mix of things—cupboard doors slamming, that woman crying and screaming, the candle flying through the air. You remember the message I got. . . ."

"I remember," said Carrie. "I remember!"

Lisa put her hands on Carrie's shoulders.

"Go on," said Dr. Miles.

Brian looked around the table. "The slamming doors were caused by Myra Halston. Why? Because Ellen McCormack had beaten her to the punch. Instead of a message of welcome, Ellen was going to give us a message of warning. That infuriated Dr. Miles's mother, who wanted Carrie to stay. So she tried to interrupt the message."

"That's it!" cried Dr. Miles. "Ellen is warning us away because she's afraid for Carrie. My mother is welcoming us here because she's glad to have Carrie back. And both of them have our Carrie confused with the original."

"I feel like a Ping-Pong ball," said Carrie.

"So what do we do now?" asked Lisa.

"You've solved the mystery," said Brian. "Get out!"

"We've solved the mystery," said Dr. Miles. "But we haven't solved the problem. There's work to be done here!"

Lisa looked worried. "Gramma, what are you talking about?"

Dr. Miles looked grim. "I intend to have a little chat with my mother."

Lisa put down her cards with a sigh. That was her third foolish bid in ten minutes. She could tell that Brian, playing as her partner, was getting frustrated. But she just couldn't concentrate. How he was able to keep his mind on the game was more than she could understand.

The clock struck eleven.

"I suppose unless we stir them up ourselves, nothing will happen till after midnight," said Dr. Miles.

"I don't think we should try to rouse them," said Carrie, throwing the ace of hearts into the center of the table. "They're doing just fine on their own."

"So are you!" said Brian. He scowled as he tossed

down the king she had forced. "I didn't know I was going to be playing with a bridge shark tonight."

Carrie laughed. "I told you I would make a better partner than Lisa. Cards and romance don't mix."

"The same goes for smart mouths," said Dr. Miles as she trumped in and took the trick.

Lisa tried to relax. She couldn't tell if the others were enjoying the game as much as they seemed to be, or if they were simply better at pretending than she was.

She was glad Brian was still here. He had had to leave to help his father for a while that afternoon, but had come back for supper, with permission from his mother to stay late.

An odd tension seemed to fill the air. They were all afraid. Yet they were confident that they were not really in danger. Lisa looked at her grandmother and marveled at how calm she seemed. How was it possible, when she was planning to confront her own mother's ghost in another hour?

But her unflappable nature was what had earned her the nickname The Great Stone Face to begin with. Lisa envied her grandmother's calm and courage, and wondered if she would ever be like that.

She smiled to herself. She had to admit that part of her was looking forward to whatever was going to happen. She had a feeling that in a confrontation between her grandmother and a ghost, the ghost wouldn't stand a chance.

So why was she, Lisa, so nervous? It wasn't just fear. She had had a strange feeling all night long, a restless itchiness, almost like having a spot that needed scratching, not on her skin, but on her soul.

"Forget it, Burton," she ordered herself. "Concentrate on the game."

They were seated at the card table in the living room. Behind Brian, facing her, was the big grandfather clock that marked the hours for them. She almost wished it weren't there. It left her acutely aware of the passage of time. Or the lack of it. The hands seemed to have stopped. She was amazed when the quarter hour finally struck. An exchange of nervous glances passed around the table. But the game continued.

At eleven-thirty it began to fall apart, with all of them making more senseless plays than logical ones.

At eleven forty-five Alice Miles threw down her cards and said, "This is nonsense. Let's just wait for midnight."

The three young people nodded in agreement, and all eyes focused on the clock as the hands crawled slowly, inexorably, toward the witching hour. Outside the wind was rising. Lisa could see the full moon through the picture window.

Brian drummed his fingers nervously on the table. Dr. Miles reached out to stop him.

The clock began to chime midnight.

Dr. Miles turned off the lamp.

Lisa felt her skin begin to crawl. Something was wrong; very wrong. She had known it all along. Things weren't as simple as everyone had thought. There was more to this than . . .

She lost her train of thought. The clock was still chiming. She looked around the table, catching the eyes of each of the others, who were doing the same thing.

The chimes stopped.

Nothing had happened.

For a long time no one spoke. When Carrie did start to say something, Dr. Miles reached out and put a hand on her arm, cautioning her to remain quiet.

The silence continued.

"Maybe they're waiting for *us*," said Brian at last.

"Shhh."

Lisa felt small droplets of sweat begin to form under her arms, along her shoulders, behind her neck. The waiting was driving her mad. "Come on!" she wanted to shout. "If you're going to come, get it over with!"

Nothing.

The clock struck the quarter hour.

"Mother always was late," said Dr. Miles. She turned on the lamp. "Perhaps we had better try the writing. I can't wait much longer. And I certainly can't go through another night like this one!"

Lisa sighed. So her grandmother *was* human! That seemed like a relief in itself. "I'll get the paper," she said. Normally Carrie would have leaped up to do it, but Lisa knew her sister had no intention of separating herself from the group now, whether the lights were on or off.

She headed for the kitchen, where they had left the pencils and paper they were using earlier that day. As soon as she entered the kitchen, she felt her skin begin to crawl again.

Suddenly she clutched the sides of her head. She tried to scream, but no sound came out. Trembling violently, she staggered and fell against the counter.

A moment later, Lisa stood and shook herself.

Her face grim and intent, she opened one of the kitchen drawers and began searching for what she needed.

12

"**H**ere we go," said Lisa brightly as she reentered the living room a few minutes later. She was carrying several pencils in her left hand. She was also clutching a large blue notebook against her chest.

Her right hand was hidden behind the notebook.

A strange light glowed in her eyes—a light that grew brighter as she drew near the table.

"Dear God!" cried Brian suddenly. Lunging against the table, he pushed Carrie and her chair over sideways. At the same moment Lisa uttered a bloodcurdling scream and swung the butcher knife she was clutching downward in a vicious arc.

Alice Miles cried out in terror. The butcher knife, which had been intended for Carrie, quivered in the tabletop. The savage strength of the blow had thrust it through the cards, the cloth, and the table itself.

As Lisa tried to wrench the knife free, Brian grabbed her by the hair, spun her around, and slapped her face. "Stop it!" he roared.

"Gramma!" screamed Carrie. "Gramma, make her stop!"

Lisa was hissing and spitting, scratching at Brian like a rabid cat. "Let me go!" she screamed as she raked her fingers down his cheek, leaving four bloody welts.

Brian slapped her again. "Get out of there!" he shouted. "You get out of Lisa's body!"

Lisa's eyes were rolling wildly.

Brian pinned her arms to her side and shook her savagely. "Get out! *Get out!*"

She tried to bite him, spittle flying from the corners of her mouth.

"Make it stop!" cried Carrie, clinging to her grandmother. "Gramma, make it stop!"

Suddenly Lisa broke free of Brian's grasp. With a screech she lunged at Carrie, her fingers straining for her little sister's neck. When Dr. Miles intercepted Lisa, grabbing her by the shoulder, Lisa lashed out and slapped her grandmother so fiercely it seemed her jaw might be broken.

Dr. Miles slapped back. "Mother!" she said, her voice firm and strong. She was gasping, and her shoulders were shaking, yet she managed to sound like a parent disciplining an unruly child. "Mother, get out of there. You don't belong."

Lisa's eyes rolled in her head. Her hair was tangled, her nostrils flaring.

Carrie turned away and threw up.

Suddenly Lisa's eyes rolled back in her head, so that only the whites showed. She convulsed wildly, as if an electric shock were running through her, then collapsed like a tent in a windstorm.

"Help me get her onto the couch," snapped Dr. Miles. She had taken Lisa's arms. Brian was just reaching for her feet when from the air above them came a cry of horror.

"Carrie!" screamed the voice. "Oh, my God! Carrie!"

At the sound Lisa opened her eyes and shuddered. The voice carried such grief and terror that she could feel tears spring to her eyes, her sympathy for the maddened creature that haunted the night even stronger than the fear that was raging through her.

The ceiling began to drip, not in one place but in several. Rank drops of green water struck the table, the couch, the carpet.

When the water turned to blood, Carrie buried her face in her arms and began to weep.

"Come on!" snapped Brian. "We're getting out of here!"

He grabbed Lisa and started for the door. A wild shriek of dismay rang out above them. Just as Brian and Lisa reached the door, it blew inward, as if struck by a mighty wind. The edge of the door caught Brian's head, and he crumpled to the floor, unconscious. Lisa grabbed at the door. It wrenched out of her fingers and slammed shut again. She tried to open it. It was jammed. Placing a foot against the wall, she yanked furiously, shaking her head from side to side.

The door would not budge.

A lamp sailed past her, missing her head by inches. It smashed on the wall above the door. Shards of pottery rained down around her.

"Brian!" she cried, dropping to her knees beside him. "Brian, are you all right?"

He made no answer.

She lifted his head into her lap. He moaned and tried to open his eyes. Suddenly Carrie shrieked. Turning toward her sister, Lisa cried out with new terror. The closet under the stairs had opened like a hungry mouth, and Carrie was being dragged toward it by some unseen force. Dr. Miles had her arms locked around Carrie's shoulders and was straining to hold her. But the force was so great that Carrie's body was stretched out parallel to the floor. One of her shoes slipped off and flew straight into the closet, as if it had been sucked in by some gigantic vacuum cleaner. Carrie's other shoe came off. A sock peeled off after it. Both disappeared into the closet.

Lisa leaped up. She could feel the force sucking at her, too. Skirting the edges of it, working desperately to avoid stepping too close, she made a large circle around the living room and came up next to the closet. Standing behind the door she began to push against it, trying to close it, to block the horrendous force within.

She let out a little gasp as something brushed against her, then realized it was Brian. He was standing behind her, his face taut, a large purple welt above one eye.

"Push!" he gasped.

Working together, the two strained desperately to close the door.

Dr. Miles was weakening, losing her grip on Carrie. She looked up.

"Daddy!" she cried. "Daddy, help me!"

Confusion seemed to explode around them—a

cacophony of shrieks and cries and noises that could not be understood.

And then everything was silent. Carrie dropped to the floor. Lisa and Brian, suddenly pushing against nothing, slammed the door so violently it jarred them. Alice Miles knelt beside Carrie, rubbing her arms and weeping.

Brian took Dr. Miles by the arm and pulled her to her feet. "You get Carrie," he snapped at Lisa. "There's no time to waste."

Lisa helped Carrie to her feet. The four of them stumbled toward the door. But when they reached it, a roar of rage split the air and the door began to slam back and forth again.

Dr. Miles straightened up a little. Shaking Brian's hands away, she said, "It's no use. She's not going to let us out."

As if in verification, the window shades came rolling down with a snap, the curtains were pulled shut across the windows, and the telephone lifted from its little table to go sailing through the air, wrenching its cord from the wall as it did.

They were trapped.

Somewhere above them a high voice began to laugh, a light, rippling laugh that should have been lovely but wasn't, because of what lay lurking behind it.

And suddenly Lisa realized what had happened, what was wrong with their plans, why they had made a dreadful, dreadful error and were now in mortal danger.

It was not that the house was haunted.

It was not that the ghost of Myra Halston wished them harm.

It was that Myra Halston was totally, terrifyingly insane.

Lisa knew this beyond a shadow of a doubt because Myra Halston was trying to get back into her head.

Grabbing for Brian's hand, she cried, "Tie me down!"

Brian turned to her, his face incredulous.

"No time for questions!" shrieked Lisa, pulling at her hair, as if that could keep the ghost out. "Tie me down before it's too late! She wants Carrie, and she's using me to get her!"

She closed her eyes and began to shake. Brian slammed her into a chair and yanked his belt free from the loops, ready to use it to bind her.

Suddenly Lisa sighed. "Wait," she said, putting a hand on his shoulder. "It's all right. She's gone."

That was true. "She" *was* gone. But the "she" in question was Lisa Burton. Her body was now completely under the control of the insane spirit of Myra Halston.

13

*L*isa wanted to scream. She had to warn the others what was happening. But she couldn't. Myra wouldn't let her.

Through eyes no longer her own, Lisa watched with horror as the others accepted what Myra was telling them—that she had fended off the attacking spirit and knew it to be gone for good.

"Don't believe her!" Lisa tried to yell. "She's lying! She's crazy!"

But she had no mouth with which to scream. The words were trapped inside.

Two spirits occupying one space made a strange overlap; somehow her mind had linked with Myra's when the woman's spirit entered her body. Now Lisa knew what Myra was thinking.

And what she was thinking was insane. Her

thoughts were shifting wildly, out of any rational control. In one moment she was planning to murder Carrie in order to bring her to the other side so they could be together. In the next she was plotting to stay in Lisa's body forever, so she could be with Carrie in life.

In either case it was Carrie who was uppermost in the woman's mind. In fact, Lisa soon realized Myra was obsessed with Carrie—obsessed not only with her death but also with something that had happened the day she died. Something that had been hidden ever since.

As the seconds ticked by, Lisa felt herself being submerged in Myra's mind. She struggled against it. She wanted to get out—*had* to get out to protect her family.

But she couldn't. Myra had the strength of insanity and Lisa was trapped.

The feeling was maddening.

Maddening? She flinched from the word, afraid she would soon be mad herself. The prospect terrified her.

Because to be Myra Halston was a terrible fate.

Lisa could see that more and more clearly. This was a mind controlled by terror.

Suddenly her own terror scaled up to a new level. *She couldn't see!* Myra had taken such total control of her body that her eyes and ears no longer sent her any information.

Fear swelled within her. She realized that if she should totally succumb to Myra, it would be a true death; her spirit would be pushed out of her body forever.

She thought of something she had heard about dreams: If you dreamed you were falling from a great height, you had to wake before you struck, or you would die in your sleep. She sensed something like that now; if she were to be overtaken by Myra's personal demons, it would be the end of her—and possibly of Carrie, too, since there would be no one left to stop whatever Myra Halston decided to do. Lisa *had* to help Carrie. But how?

Perhaps if she understood Myra Halston better....

She thought suddenly of the title of the song she had listened to so many times that summer: "The Corridors of My Mind." What if she traveled the corridors of Myra's mind? Could she find the key to breaking Myra's control over her?

She took a mental step forward, cautious, hesitant. She knew that as surely as the spirit of Myra Halston haunted their house, so Myra Halston herself was haunted by demons of her own making. And Lisa was afraid to meet them.

She wanted to go back. But how could she do that? She had no place to go back to. Myra had her body, and she herself was lost in Myra's mind.

Lisa shivered—or at least, she felt the feeling that would have caused a shiver if she still had a body of her own.

Somewhere she heard weeping.

That made sense. Myra had been weeping for sixty years now. The sound of it must echo through every twist and turn of her soul.

Lisa began to walk. To her right she saw a door. Where had it come from? Was she imagining it? Or had the thought of corridors made it appear, like some living metaphor, a tangible symbol of what she was looking for?

Feeling as if she was walking through a dream, Lisa approached the door. Terrified of what she might find

125

on the other side, she hesitated, then forced herself to open it.

Inside was the ocean shore on a beautiful moonlit night. Waves surged across the sand. A warm breeze rustled through a young man's hair. A full moon flooded the beach with whiteness.

Lisa backed away, closing the door gently.

But she felt a little better. It was good to know that not all of Myra's memories were of sorrow or madness.

Behind another door she found Myra's wedding day, and a strange mix of feelings, joy and terror and pride and hope all jumbled together in a mixture of white lace and flowers.

Some doors led to blackness, as if the memories had been forced from Myra's mind, leaving only emptiness in their place. Others led to quiet scenes of family life.

It was when she opened the seventh door that she began to scream. No sooner had she stepped through it than clammy hands reached out to touch her, groping across her face, her arms, her body.

She slammed the door shut and leaned against it, panting and shaking. Looking back where she had come from, she wondered what her grandmother would do if she were here.

She knew the answer at once. She would go on and open every door she could, no matter how frightening the prospect, until she found something that might help.

Lisa knew she had to do the same thing. She had a problem, so she had to study it to solve it. But she had never had to learn in a library like this—a library of memories, where the pages could reach out and grab you by the throat.

She squared her shoulders and opened another door.

Candles. A million candles. And in the center of the room, dressed in white, the dead body of a beautiful little girl.

Lisa choked back a sob.

This must be Carrie Halston.

She stepped into the room and threaded her way through the candles. The tiny body lay on an altar draped in green and gold. The hands were folded on her chest and her tightly curled hair was carefully arranged around her neck and shoulders.

Daisies lay scattered at her feet.

The child's face was soft and peaceful. Lisa looked down at the girl who would have been her great-aunt. She could see a hint of *her* Carrie in the face—the snub nose, the high cheekbones. She reached out, then drew her hand back with a gasp.

The eyes had snapped open.

"Mommy?"

The smell of pond water filled the air.

Suddenly the little girl's hair was no longer curled, but wet and lank, clinging to her shoulders. "Mommy!" she cried. "Mommy, where are you? I need you!" The voice was edged with hysteria.

The girl turned toward Lisa, her eyes wide, twice as wide as any eyes could ever be, her face distorted with a terrible accusing anger. Her mouth opened to show great dripping fangs, green algae clinging in the gaps.

"You weren't there!" The cry was a deep, rasping roar. *"You weren't there!"*

And then she lunged.

Lisa turned and ran screaming through the room. She knocked down candles, hundreds of candles, which blazed and flared as they hit the floor. The room became an inferno behind her. And walking through the fire, clothes ablaze, hair in flames, eyes wide and staring, was the girl who had lain on the altar.

"Join me in death," she crooned. "Join me in death, Mommy."

Lisa screamed again and ran forward.

A door!

She pulled up short. There was something wrong with the door. It was a bad door, a frightening door. Somehow Lisa knew it had never been opened and that it was never supposed to be opened. Myra Halston had sealed it more than fifty years ago, locked it in the deepest and most terrified part of her mind and done everything she could to forget it was there.

But it *was* there.

And it was the only way out.

But what was on the other side?

Lisa looked behind her. The fire was raging out of control. The little figure was almost on her, flaming hands reaching for her, fangs working hungrily.

She turned back to the door. Her hesitation ended when she felt a burning hand on her leg. With a scream, she flung open the door and leaped through.

14

She was in a garden.

She wrinkled her brow. Why would such a beautiful place be sealed away so deep in Myra's mind, as if it were the greatest horror of all?

She looked around and flinched when she saw Carrie again. But this was a different Carrie, lively and vibrant, a lovely young girl wearing a frilly dress. She was sitting on a swing under a towering tree. It took Lisa a moment, but she recognized the tree—it was a younger version of one that still stood in what was left of the backyard.

From the house she could hear the sound of a gramophone playing "Beautiful Dreamer."

Carrie seemed not to notice her.

Lisa began to walk forward. Following a path that wound through the plantings, she soon passed a fish pond. She shivered and went on.

Ahead of her she could see a white, wooden summerhouse, lacy and latticed. Inside was a large swing. Sitting side by side on the swing were a young man and a beautiful woman. Their gay laughter was like music in the air.

Like Carrie, they did not seem to notice Lisa.

She walked to the edge of the summerhouse and peered in through the latticed wall. The woman was her great-grandmother. She had lovely auburn hair, coiled on her head. She wore a white dress that had frills at the cuffs and down the front. She was extraordinarily beautiful, in an ethereal sort of way. It was obvious that the young man thought so. He was clearly infatuated with her.

The man turned to Lisa and looked her in the eye.

She gasped. A flood of information poured into her mind. She put her hand to her throat, needing time to digest what she was learning. She wasn't sure how the information was coming to her. But she was sure that she now knew as much about the young man as Myra did.

His name was Andrew Long. He worked for Harrison Halston, Myra's husband. He was also in awe of Harrison, whom he took to be everything he had ever dreamed of becoming himself.

Andrew Long was from a poor family that had scrounged for food and clothing during the years of his childhood. His father had died in the first World War. His mother had worked two jobs to bring in food. Andrew had left school and begun work when he was twelve. He was tough, smart, and hungry—hungry for life, hungry for security, hungry for love.

He had come to Harrison Halston's office as a messenger boy ten years earlier and risen slowly but steadily to a position of trust and power, because tough, smart, and hungry was just the way Harrison Halston liked his employees.

Only Andrew Long was a little too tough, a little too smart, and a little too hungry. Worst of all, he was a little too fearful of losing all he had gained.

And he had good reason to be afraid, because he had done something terribly stupid. He had fallen in love with Harrison Halston's greatest treasure, the delicate, half-mad Myra. Perhaps it was because he walked the thin edge of sanity himself that something in him reached out to her. But he was sane enough to know that what he was doing was crazy, that he was playing with something worse than fire when he began to pursue her. And that he would have to do an awfully good job of covering his tracks, or risk losing his newfound status.

Myra Halston had thought little of Andrew Long's attention at first. Oh, she was mildly flattered. But she was used to men falling in love with her; it had been going on most of her life. So she toyed with Andrew, flirting and smiling in a way she thought was innocent, not knowing she was weaving a web that would doom them all.

Andrew Long had come that day, after three sleepless nights, to declare his love for Myra Halston and to ask her to run away with him. Half mad now himself, torn between love and the knowledge that his love would cost him everything if he declared it, he had come to declare it anyway—only to have it laughingly rebuffed by Myra.

And in a moment, when Carrie Halston would step from the bushes and see him trying to kiss her mother,

Andrew Long would fall over that thin line between sanity and madness, and pass from lover to murderer.

Lisa let out a gasp of fear.

It was happening. It was happening now, and there was nothing she could do to stop it.

From a clump of bushes beside the summerhouse, Lisa watched the delicate girl step forward. She carried a handful of daisies. The sleeve of her white dress was stained with something green.

"Carrie!" cried Myra Halston.

Andrew Long leaped up, a horrible look of panic in his eyes. He started toward the summerhouse door. Toward Carrie.

The girl screamed at the look on his face, then turned and began running down the path.

Myra stood, her eyes wide with fright. She started after them, stumbled over her long dress, and lost consciousness when her head struck the doorframe.

Lisa thought that would be the end of it, that the memory would end. But there was more. She could hear Carrie screaming, "Mommy! Mommy! I need you!"

Myra Halston pushed herself to her knees, then staggered to her feet. Lifting the edge of her dress, she ran down the garden path. Lisa took off after her. Side by side, Lisa and Myra reached the fish pond.

Andrew Long was kneeling at the edge of the water, his hands around Carrie's neck.

Her face was under the water, her body convulsing mightily. With the strength that sometimes comes when death is near, she wrenched herself out of the water. "Mommy!" she screamed. *"Mommy!"*

Andrew Long plunged her face back into the pond.

Myra Halston, too fragile for the real world and far, far too delicate for this, fainted.

Somewhere in the distance the gramophone continued to play "Beautiful Dreamer."

And then Lisa was gone, ejected not only from Myra Halston's mind, but from her own body.

But just before that happened, she pulled two more pieces of information about Andrew Long from the mind of Myra Halston.

The first was that, in spite of her denials, even to herself, until that day in the garden Myra had truly loved Andrew Long.

The second was that two days after he murdered Carrie Halston, the guilt-stricken Andrew Long had taken the pistol his father had left him and used it to blow his own brains out.

Lisa was floating. She looked around. She saw nothing above, or below, or anywhere. It was as if she had been lifted into the night sky and left to drift in a vast and endless darkness.

She began to weep. Would she be lost here forever?

"There, there, lass," said a voice beside her. "It's not that bad, is it?"

Lisa looked around. The voice seemed to have come from nowhere.

"Who are you?" she asked in a whisper. "I can't see you."

"Just a moment," said the voice. "I'll try to fix that. You try, too."

Lisa was about to ask what she was supposed to try when another voice, deep and gravelly, said, "All right, Ellen. But I'm not sure I can manage it."

Something began to ripple in the mist beside her.

Slowly a form began to appear. As Lisa watched, the face of a jolly-looking woman took shape. She was dressed in a robe that appeared somewhat tattered. Colorless, translucent, she was nevertheless clearly visible to Lisa now.

"My name is Ellen McCormack," she said. "I've been trying to talk to you for days."

There was a motion beside Ellen, and another figure appeared. Tall and lean, he wore an elegant dressing gown and what appeared to be a permanent scowl. He was not as good at materialization as Ellen McCormack was; Lisa could see him only out of the corners of her eyes. When she looked at him straight on, he disappeared.

"Hello, Lisa," he said gruffly. "I'm glad to meet you. I apologize for the circumstances."

"Hello, Great-grandfather," she said softly. "I'm glad to meet you, too."

She looked at Ellen McCormack. The diversion created by the arrival of the two ghosts had briefly beaten down her panic. Now it rose full force again. "Where am I?" she cried.

"You're in-between," said Ellen McCormack. "In the place where the dead are trapped when they haven't freed themselves from Earth. We need to talk to you."

"Am I dead?" asked Lisa. A strange calm passed over her. For a moment it didn't seem to matter if she was dead, though somewhere within her she could sense something struggling against the idea.

"Oh, my, no," Ellen McCormack laughed. "You, dead? Perish the thought!" Her voice became serious. "But you are in danger, child, and we had to communicate with you. Bringing you here was the only way we knew how. We have to tell you about Mrs. Halston."

"You must understand her," said Mr. Halston.

"Yes," said Ellen. "You see, Mrs. Halston is a strong spirit. You wouldn't think it of someone who's gone mad like she has. But she's stronger than either of us."

"It's the madness that gives her strength," said Mr. Halston. "She was the strongest one of all of us, though we never knew it. She bent the whole household to her will—even after her death."

He shook his head sadly.

"That's the truth," said Ellen McCormack. "It's a terrible thing she's done to us. A terrible thing indeed."

"What has she done?"

"Keep us here! Kept us while she longed for her precious Carrie. Not that I blame her. My heart ached for the child, too. But Mrs. Halston is confused. Somehow she thinks Carrie is still on Earth, still to be found among the living. That's why she got so stirred up when your sister came along."

"I don't quite follow all this," said Lisa.

"Let me try, Ellen," said Mr. Halston.

"As you like, sir."

Lisa's great-grandfather was silent for a moment. "It's very confusing to die," he said at last. "In a way, it's almost like being born. Everything is different again. Some people handle it very well. Others ... don't take it well at all."

Lisa could sense him looking for a way to help her understand.

"We don't belong here," he said after a moment. "This place, this nothingness, is like a train station—

just a stop on the journey. After you die you have to let go of the physical world before you can go all the way to the other side, which is where you really belong.

"Most people make the transition sooner or later. But a troubled spirit, someone who can't let go of the mortal world for one reason or another, isn't able to make that passage.

"That's what a ghost is. Some spirit who has been trapped here because he or she hasn't been able to let go of the connections to the physical world.

"Myra is that way. She longed for Carrie so desperately that she never really accepted her death. So she continued to look for her in your world, even after she herself had died. That's why the house is haunted."

"What about you?" asked Lisa. "Why are you still here?"

"We're bound to her," Ellen McCormack said bitterly. "She's stronger than we are."

Harrison Halston put a hand on Ellen's shoulder. Though neither of them was solid, Lisa found the gesture oddly moving.

"Don't hold it against her, Ellen," he said softly. "She can't help herself."

"Oh, I know that." She sighed. "But I am everlastingly weary of this place. I want to move on. The problem is," she said, turning to Lisa, "Mrs. Halston's spiritual energies have bound us to her. We were tied together anyway, all three of us dying in that fire as we did." She shuddered, as if more than half a century later the memory was still painful. "When we got to this place, I was ready to keep going. So was Mr. Halston. But not her. Oh, no. She would have none of it. 'Not without Carrie!' she cried. 'I can't go on without Carrie!' And that's the saddest part of the whole mess. Carrie isn't down here. And she isn't in-between. She's the only one of us who's gone on to the other side where she belongs."

Ellen McCormack shook her head. "All this time Mrs. Halston has been looking in the wrong place. If she would just go on herself, if she'd just let things go along as they're supposed to, it would all work out fine. You can't fight these things. You have to let them happen."

"Where *is* Carrie?" asked Lisa.

"I told you. She's on the other side."

"How do you get there?"

"You just ... go. When you're ready, you just kind of drift over. I saw it happen once. There was this glow, this lovely light. And then this spirit who had been roaming around suddenly let go all his ties to the old world and just swooped through that light." Her look was distant and dreamy now. "It was—oh, I can't tell you. But it was wonderful. I think of it all the time. Long for it." She looked at Lisa sadly.

Lisa could sense the woman's sorrow, and ached to help her.

"You do that well, you know," said Ellen McCormack.

Lisa blinked. "What do you mean?"

"Sense people's feelings. You have a natural talent for it. That's why you made contact so easily the first time you tried the writing—and why Myra was able to zero in on you. You have a natural ..." She looked frustrated. "What's that word, Harrison?"

"Empathy," said Lisa's great-grandfather. "She's naturally empathetic. Too empathetic for her own good." He turned to Lisa. "You should also learn to

137

pay more attention. We went out of our way to warn you. I played the piano with Myra last night just to distract her while Ellen tried to communicate with you. Ellen got the message through. But you ignored it."

Lisa started to protest. Harrison Halston raised his hand. "I know, I know. That was mostly your grandmother's fault." He shook his head. "My dear little Alice was like her mother that way. Stubborn."

"She's done well, though," Ellen said proudly.

"I don't care how well she's done!" cried Lisa. "What are *we* going to do? How am I going to get back into my body?"

"I don't know," Ellen said sadly. "Mrs. Halston is awfully strong. And she wants Carrie."

"Carrie!" cried Lisa. "That's it! What if we got Carrie for her? The first Carrie, I mean."

Her great-grandfather looked puzzled. "What are you talking about?"

"Couldn't we call Carrie back from wherever she's gone? Then Myra would leave us alone."

Ellen looked at her thoughtfully. "I don't know," she said. "I never heard of anyone coming back. I guess it wouldn't hurt to try. We'd best join forces, though." She reached out and took Lisa's left hand. Harrison Halston reached for her right.

Suddenly Lisa felt warm. She was linked to Ellen and to her great-grandfather. She found thoughts intruding on her—bits and pieces of information, traces of memory, scraps of dreams and longings drifting in from both of them.

Lisa gasped. She wasn't sure she liked this. If she could sense their thoughts and feelings, surely they could sense hers. If she could have blushed, she would have. There were a lot of things in her mind she certainly didn't want her great-grandfather to know!

Then there was no time to think.

"Carrie!" cried Ellen. "Carrie, can you hear us?"

She didn't cry out with her voice; she called with her mind.

Harrison Halston began to call, too. "Carrie, can you hear us?"

Lisa could sense his call following Ellen McCormack's, winding around it like a vine, following it and strengthening it.

"Carrie!" called Lisa. "Carrie, can you hear us?"

It was not simply a call. It was a longing, a need. Merged with her great-grandfather and Ellen, she sensed their great love for the child and the enormous aching sorrow they had felt when she died.

"Carrie!" they cried. "Carrie, can you hear us?"

No answer.

"Carrie. Carrie, Carrie, Carrie!" The call echoed through infinity, seeking Carrie Halston.

Somewhere below them another Carrie heard it.

"Here!" she cried. "I'm here! Help me!"

Lisa broke away from the others. Something was wrong!

"Carrie!" she cried again, and this time she was not crying out for a Carrie long dead, but for her own little sister.

Her Carrie was in terrible danger.

Lisa had to go to her.

15

Lisa found herself plunging down. She could sense the two spirits traveling beside her.

In an instant the three of them were in the moonlit garden behind the house.

Lisa corrected herself. They were in what was left of the garden. Having seen the original in Myra Halston's mind, she knew what a pitiful remnant this was.

But Lisa had no time to think about the garden. She had seen what was happening, and it was horrible.

Myra Halston, still controlling Lisa's body, had taken Carrie into the garden. She stood in back of her now, with one arm wrapped around her and holding her tight.

With her other hand she held the butcher knife against Carrie's throat, ready to draw it across the tender flesh.

Brian was standing about ten feet in front of her, trying to reason with her.

As Lisa watched, Alice Miles came staggering around the corner of the house. She was clutching her right arm, which hung limp and useless at her side.

Lisa wanted to stop them somehow, to make them tell her what had been going on while she had been gone. She threw herself at her own body, trying to push her way back in. It was hopeless. Myra Halston was in complete control, and Lisa could only float outside, watching helplessly.

Myra's madness had blossomed into its fullest. Lisa shivered as she heard the words that came out of her own mouth. Her voice was sweet and seductive. "It will only hurt for a moment. Then we'll be together again, Carrie. Forever and ever. Won't that be nice?"

Carrie was held tight against Lisa's body, unable to move. "Please," she whispered. "Please, let me go."

"Lisa," said Brian. "Or Myra, or whoever you are. Let go of her!" He took a step toward the two girls.

"Stand back!" screamed Myra. "Get away!"

Brian stopped in his tracks. Alice Miles staggered up beside him. "Don't aggravate her," she whispered. "There is no telling what she'll do."

Brian nodded grimly.

"It's time to come to Mommy," crooned Myra. "Oh, Carrie. Mommy has been waiting so long for this. Don't you want to be with me again? You'll feel just a little hurt, and then we'll be together forever."

Carrie was trembling violently. Myra pressed the knife more tightly against her throat. "I don't want to do it until you're ready," she murmured. "It won't be nearly so nice if I do. Haven't you missed me, darling? Haven't you missed your mother?"

Lisa read the terror in her sister's eyes and ached for her.

"Isn't there any way to stop her?" she cried, turning to the spirits who floated beside her.

Ellen McCormack was weeping. Harrison Halston's face was hard as stone. "None," he said bitterly.

"Don't you remember?" asked Myra. "Listen!" A strange look crossed her face. "Mommy?" she called in a high-pitched voice. "Mommy, where are you?"

She dropped her voice to its normal tone. "Don't you remember how you were looking for me?" she asked. "You looked and looked. And now, here I am. I've come for you at last. Oh, please, Carrie. Please say it's all right. Then I can finish it, and we can be together."

Listening to the words come from her own lips, seeing that madness shine in her own eyes, made Lisa ill.

Myra pressed the knife more tightly against Carrie's neck. A thin red line appeared beneath the blade.

"Leave me alone!" screamed Carrie. "Leave me alone!"

Myra's eyes flashed with rage. "You ungrateful child! You're not Carrie. You're not *my* Carrie at all! I'll punish you for this!"

She raised the knife and was ready to plunge it downward when Brian cried, "Myra, stop!"

She hesitated, her hand in the air.

Because it wasn't Brian.

Lisa let out a gasp. She could see Brian's spirit floating outside his body, just as she was outside hers. He looked dazed, confused.

Clearly someone had taken over his body, just as Myra had taken over hers.

But who? She looked beside her. Ellen and her great-grandfather were still there.

What was going on?

"Myra, put down the knife."

It wasn't Brian's voice. It was a voice Lisa had never heard before.

But Myra had.

"Andrew? Andrew, is that you?"

Brian took a step toward her. "Yes, Myra. It's me."

Andrew Long! The man who had murdered the first Carrie, all those years ago.

Myra twisted Lisa's face in wrath. "What do you want? Why are you here?"

"I've been here all along," replied Andrew. "Here in the garden, waiting to see you again, to tell you how sorry I am. Waiting to make up for what I did." He moved Brian's body another step in her direction. "Put down the knife, Myra."

Lisa could see Myra's hand tremble as she wavered under Andrew Long's gaze. Her fingers played back and forth on the hilt of the knife.

Brian's body took another step toward Lisa's body; Andrew Long moved in on Myra Halston.

"Put the knife down," he said again, his voice gentle but firm.

Myra began to lower the shining blade.

"That's right," said Andrew Long. "That's right, Myra." He took another step in her direction.

Lisa could see Myra struggling with herself. The body she had stolen was trembling with the effort. Brian's body took another step forward. It reached out and grabbed the arm that held the knife.

"Now, Carrie!" cried Andrew Long. "Run!"

Carrie twisted out of Myra's grasp and raced to her

143

grandmother. Lisa watched with horror as her own face was distorted by the wrath of the person in her body.

"You beast!" she cried. "You've robbed me again! You've taken my baby!"

She wrenched her hand free from his grasp. Lisa screamed as the butcher knife sliced across Brian's face, opening a wound that splattered blood in all directions.

"No!" she cried. "No! No! No!"

Myra's hand flew back. The knife was poised for another strike.

And then she heard it.

They all heard it, spirits and fleshbound alike. Every one of them looked up, straining to see where it was coming from.

It was the high, piping voice of a child. "Mommy? Mommy, where are you?"

Lisa cried out in joy as she saw a light above her; a beautiful light.

The voice came from somewhere within it.

One by one Myra Halston's fingers opened. She dropped the knife. "Carrie? Carrie, is that you?"

"Mommy, where are you? I've been waiting for you!"

A look of rapture transformed Myra Halston's face. She threw out her arms and cried in joy, "I'm coming, Carrie! I'm coming!"

There was a flash of light.

And then she was gone.

Lisa looked up into a pair of remarkably blue eyes. "Brian!"

He had his hand on the side of his face. Blood trickled between his fingers. "I'm glad you're all right," he said. "I was worried—"

That was as far as he got. His legs buckled, and he collapsed. Lisa sat up and looked around. Carrie and her grandmother stood a few feet away, looking dazed.

"Help me!" cried Lisa. "We've got to get him to the hospital."

As if waking from a trance, they walked slowly toward Lisa.

"Lisa?" asked Carrie tentatively. "Is it really you?"

"Of course it's me!" she snapped in exasperation. Then she realized why Carrie might well wonder, and said more softly, "Yes, it's really me. Myra is gone for good, sweetie. Now come on. I need your help."

They walked hesitantly forward. Lisa felt a piercing sorrow. How long would it be before her sister trusted her again? She looked at her grandmother. "What's wrong with your arm, Gramma?"

Dr. Miles scowled. "It's broken, I think. You threw me against Brian's car."

"It wasn't *me!*" cried Lisa. "Can't you see that?"

Dr. Miles frowned. "Yes. I'm sorry. That was a terrible thing to say." She looked around, as if noticing where they were for the first time. "Carrie, give your sister a hand! We've got to help Brian."

Carrie took Brian's feet. Lisa put her hands under his arms. Working together, they dragged him around the corner of the house. Brian's car was blocking theirs, so rather than move his car and then have to hunt for the keys to their own car, Lisa decided to use his. She searched in his pants pockets and found the keys. Then they managed to get Brian into the backseat.

They squeezed Dr. Miles in back, too. She clutched her useless arm, pain glazing her eyes. Lisa closed the door for her. "It'll be all right, Gramma," she whispered. "We'll get it taken care of soon."

Lisa walked around the car and closed the other door. It turned her stomach to see the gaping wound on Brian's handsome face. Myra's knife had done its work well. Lisa shuddered. She wondered how many stitches he would require.

She glanced across at her grandmother. Dr. Miles nodded weakly.

Lisa went to the front of the car and slid in behind the steering wheel. She only had a learner's permit. But she had a feeling there would be no problem with the police if they should stop her. She had plenty of reason to be heading for the hospital.

She looked beside her and felt tears spring out in her eyes. Carrie was cowering against the passenger door, her face twisted by a look of terror.

"Hey, Carrie, it's all over," she said, reaching out to her sister.

Carrie began to scream. "Don't touch me!" she cried. "Don't touch me! Don't touch me! Don't touch me!"

Tears streaming down her face, Lisa headed for the hospital.

EPILOGUE

Lisa stamped the snow off her feet.

"Mail call!" she cried, throwing her hat onto the brass rack in the foyer.

"Anything for me?" asked her mother. She was sitting at the kitchen table, studying the textbook for her computer-programming course.

"Two bills," said Lisa. "And an advertisement wanting you to subscribe to *Modern Motorcycling*."

Mrs. Burton made a face. "Thanks a lot. Next time don't bother."

"I don't write 'em, I just deliver 'em," said Lisa with a smile.

"How about me?" asked Carrie.

"Not a thing."

"Look at her grinning!" said Carrie. "You and I didn't make out so well, Mom, but I bet I can tell you one letter that's in that pile."

"That doesn't take a mental giant," said Mrs. Burton. "She gets one every day. Like clockwork."

"Ha!" said Lisa. "You're just jealous. Both of you."

She headed up the stairs to her room. She had just settled into the chair at her desk when she heard Carrie say, "Will you read me some of it? Not the mushy parts. Just any news."

Lisa turned around. Carrie was standing in her doorway. Though Lisa didn't say a thing she felt a surge of elation. This was the first time Carrie had come into her room since they had returned from Sayers Island more than six months ago.

The first two months had been awful. Carrie would hardly go near Lisa. And the first time their parents had left the sisters alone together, Carrie had begun to scream as if she were being attacked. Mrs. Burton had rushed back to find Carrie in a corner, huddling in terror, and Lisa standing helplessly in the center of the room, tears streaming down her face.

It had taken months of patient talking and careful overtures to get Carrie out of her state of constant fear. Lisa knew she would carry the effects of what had happened on the island for the rest of her life.

But she was making progress. That was good.

"I said, will you read me part of it?" repeated Carrie.

Lisa smiled. "Sure. Have a seat, squirt."

Carrie walked over to Lisa's desk. Lisa could sense her sister's nervousness. It hurt to see her that way. But she knew she had to be patient.

She opened the envelope and scanned the front side of the letter.

"Well, everything's fine," she said. "Is that what you wanted to know?"

"Lisa!"

Lisa smiled. "Okay, I'll give you some details. 'Dear Lisa. I miss you more than . . .' Well, you don't need to hear that. Let's see. Second paragraph. 'Every night before I go to sleep . . .' No, that's not really news, either. Hmm. There must be something here that would be of interest to you."

She glanced in her sister's direction. Carrie was grinning. But she was also beginning to look quite exasperated.

Lisa turned the letter over and let out a shriek of delight.

"What is it?" cried Carrie. "What does it say?"

"Oh, nothing much," said Lisa, a grin splitting her face. "I'll read it to you. Ahem. 'I got an interesting piece of mail the other day. It was a letter from Burnham College. My application has been accepted, and they've granted me a scholarship that will just about cover what my parents and I aren't able to come up with. Do you think you can stand it if I spend the next four years in your neighborhood?' It's signed, 'Love, Scarface.' "

Carrie sighed. "Gosh, that's so romantic."

Lisa laughed. "Come on, twerp. I'll play you a game of Monopoly."

SPIRIT WORLD
SPIRITS AND SPELLS

Bruce Coville

Trying out their new haunted house game, Spirits and Spells, in a real old haunted house seemed like a good idea to Tansy, Travis and their friends. But that was before they found out what was in the attic . . . and the basement . . . and everywhere in between . . .

Now they must play the game as though their lives depend on it – because they do . . . .

Another Hodder Children's book

SPIRIT WORLD
EYES OF THE TAROT

Bruce Coville

When Bonnie McBurnie begins to use the ancient deck of tarot cards she found in her grandmother's attic, she taps into a power unlike anything she's ever imagined.

Soon the ancient forces of the tarot begin to haunt Bonnie's life, forcing her to face a fearful secret buried in her own past – and the terrifying wrath of a powerful sorcerer who has been waiting centuries for his chance to return.

Can Bonnie master the cards – or will their strange power destroy not only her, but everyone she loves?

Another Hodder Children's book

SPIRIT WORLD
CREATURE OF FIRE

Bruce Coville

The night before her death, Marilyn's eccentric Aunt Zenobia asks her to care for an ancient amulet. But her aunt is handing her more than just a strange piece of jewellery – she's handing her a passport to a terrifying new world. And it may be a one way trip. Faced with an ancient curse, a tragic demon and a blood feud thousands of years old, Marilyn must make the right decision – or die . . .